VOICES III

VOICES III

An Anthology of Fiction Written in 2009

High Hill Press. USA

Published by High Hill Press, Missouri

HighHillPress@aol.com
www.highhillpressreview.com

First High Hill edition: 2010
10 9 8 7 6 5 4 3 2 1

Cover designed by High Hill Press Art Division
ISBN: 978-1-60653-022-1
Library of Congress Number in publication data.

Table of Contents

Xs and Os

    By Jan Morrill   9

A Love that Lasts

    By Delois McGrew, Louella Turner

    & Regina Williams   17

The Fate of Tate

    By Brenda Brinkley   33

The Sound of Death

    By Erin York   41

Justice

    By Duke Pennell   49

Not What I Expected

    By Steve Whisnant   61

Tim, the Radar Man

    By Ralph H. Herron   69

The Coon Hunting Contest

    By Nancy Hartney   75

More Than Fruitcake

    By Nancy Hartney   87

Changes

    By Alan Zacher   95

The Goldfish Tattoo

  By Susan Varno   105

The Good Lord Giveth

  By Dusty Richards   115

The Red Quilt

  By Georgia Alderink   125

Bonds of Matrimony

  By M. Carolyn Steele   135

Hide and Seek

  By Velda Brotherton   139

The Flying Fuquas

  By Jerrel Swingle   151

Maurice's Gift

  By Patty Stith   159

Savant

  By Rochelle Wisoff-Fields   167

A Change of Mind

  By Ann Holbrook   177

Sack of Suckers

  By Russell Gayer   183

Congratulations to Jan Morrill for winning Voices 2010 Fiction Award for her story Xs and Os.

Xs and Os
By Jan Morrill

*T*he sun was a white ball against the blue sky, and it beat down on Jubie Lee's black skin like a flame against Auntie Bess's cast iron skillet. She stood in front of Mitchell's Five and Dime, watching hundreds of Japanese folk get off the train. The men wiped their brows with hankies, and ladies followed behind, carrying crying babies. Their older kids tagged along close by, holding on to their Mama's skirts.

They was a strange-looking bunch, all right. Sure didn't look like they belonged in Arkansas. Least she'd never seen none like them around her parts before. The *Arkansas Gazette* said something about them being sent here from California. For their own protection, it said. But Uncle Joe said it was to keep them from spying on the United States while the war was going on.

Heck. These folks didn't look like no spies. Least not the kind Jubie had seen in the movies. She felt kinda sorry for them, being taken from their homes and all. She remembered what it was like to have to leave her home when Mama couldn't pay the rent no more after Daddy was killed. And, she knew what it was liked to be stared at by folks who didn't want you around.

A crowd gathered around to watch the prisoners—Japs some called them. White folk paced on one side of the track, like buzzards flying around a dead animal. Blacks gathered on the other side.

9

A few men in the white crowd started yelling. "Go home! We don't want your kind around here."

Them words might as well have been rocks thrown at Jubie. She moved closer to Auntie Bess, until she realized: this time they weren't being thrown at her. She was used to that kind of ugliness, but sweet Jesus, this time the white folk was spewing words at them Japanese. No, she'd never thought about folks 'sides Negros not being wanted around 'cause of the color of their skin.

"Okay, sugar," Auntie Bess said, tugging at Jubie's pigtail. "We best head over to the camp cafeteria. These folks must be hungry."

"Yes'm." Jubie shuffled behind, kicking pebbles out of her way. Shoot. It was so dang hot in that mess hall. 'Sides, none of them Japanese ever said "hi." Never said much of anything, matter-of-fact. They'd just walk on by, sadness all over their faces. It made her sad, too. And standing behind that counter serving up food just made her wish she was at home eating supper herself.

One, two, three, four, five. Five steps she counted as she followed Auntie Bess up into the cafeteria building. The room might've hid her from the sun, but with no breeze, it was still too hot. She ran her hand along empty tables as she walked by. A dozen or so food servers milled about, uncovering big pots of what smelled like spaghetti. Did Japanese people eat spaghetti?

Today she was supposed to help Miss Barnes with the green beans. She picked up the spoon and swished them around, looking for pieces of bacon like Auntie Bess put in hers. Didn't find a single piece though.

A Japanese man peeked inside the room.

"If you hungry, you done found the right place," Auntie Bess said. "This here's the cafeteria."

He took his hat off and walked in. Reminded Jubie of when her cat, Mr. Jack would prowl around the front porch first thing in the morning, looking for ole Duke-the-hound-dog. Dozens of others shuffled in behind him.

She scooped up a spoonful of steaming green beans and plopped it onto each plate they held in front of her. Every so often, she'd smile at one of them. Sometimes they'd smile back all polite-like, and sometimes they'd just keep staring down at their plates. Not interested in being friendly this morning, she guessed. Maybe on another day.

The line stretched out the door and reminded her of the ant trail she liked to watch off her porch steps in the afternoons. One little ant following another, never straying, never stopping to say a friendly word. Couldn't even tell any of them apart. Sometimes she'd drop a bread crumb on them. Heavens. Just like dropping green beans on the Japanese folks' plates.

Then a little girl smiled at her, and it made Jubie think of all those times she'd hurried out to Auntie Bess's garden to see if anything had blossomed yet. Days and days of staring at dull, brown earth would pass. And then finally, one day there it would be, a tiny little bud peeking its head through that ugly brown soil.

"No, thank you," the little Japanese girl said, still smiling. "I don't really like green beans."

Jubie couldn't believe it. A Japanese that smiles *and* talks? "You speak American?" She rolled her eyes. Why'd she ask a stupid question like that?

"Of course I do. I was born in America. Why wouldn't I speak English?"

It didn't happen often, but Jubie couldn't think of a darn thing to say. She stared at the little girl, tongue-tied.

A lady next to the girl pushed her along. "Hurry up, Sachi. Others are waiting."

"Okay, Mama." She looked back at Jubie. "'Bye for now. Maybe I'll see you later?"

Jubie had so many questions to ask this stranger, this girl who wasn't white and wasn't black. What was it like where she lived? Was it as hot as Arkansas? What grade was she in? Did she also speak Japanese? Maybe she could teach Jubie a new language. "Sachi. Right?" She spoke quickly. Had to get it all said before Sachi moved too far down the line. "My name is Jubie Lee. Jubie for short. I'll be finished here in a few hours. Meet me at the front gate?"

"Okay! See you there," Sachi said.

Jubie couldn't wait, and for the rest of the afternoon, she didn't really care if any of the other Japanese smiled or spoke as they shuffled past her green bean station.

August days were the hottest and longest of the year. Seemed like it took darn-near forever for the sun to go down. Come to think of it, that old sun was kinda like Jubie's little brother, Troy Junior. Sometimes it seemed like he hung around just to bother her.

She'd been waiting for almost an hour. Maybe Sachi wasn't coming. She kicked the ground, stirring up a tiny dust cloud around her feet. Why wouldn't she show up? Maybe she found herself another friend. She picked up a stick and drew four crossed lines in the dirt. Tic-tac-toe. X's and O's. Not much fun, playing the silly game alone. Where was Sachi?

The answer to Jubie's question—the one she'd tried to keep locked away—busted through and tickled her stomach like that time she got sick with what Auntie Bess called the gut bug. Maybe Sachi didn't come because her mama said she couldn't play with no colored girl. She drew a line through the X's and scratched the game away.

Why'd she have to go and get her hopes up anyway? Shoulda known the Japanese would think the same way as white folk. But why did Sachi smile at her? And why did she go and say she'd meet her after lunch?

"You coming, Jubie Lee?" Auntie Bess called from outside the gate.

"You go on. I'll be right there." From behind the bob-wire fence, Jubie watched her aunt stroll down the road toward town. She rubbed her finger over one of the prickly knots that lined the fence. The helpers were allowed to leave after serving lunch, just walk on through that gate. But what about them Japanese prisoners? What was it like to have to stay behind the bob-wire?

"There you are."

Jubie spun around to find the voice. "Oh. Hi, Sachi."

The Japanese girl had changed into overalls. She pointed to the shade behind the guard shack. "I was waiting for you over there. When you didn't come, I thought you'd changed your mind. Then I saw you standing over here."

Jubie giggled. "I didn't see you. Didn't think you were coming neither."

"I thought I'd be cooler in the shade. It sure is hot here."

"Sun don't bother me none." Jubie stared at Sachi's patent leather shoes, and felt a little jealous, even though they were all dusty. She tried to pull her pinky toe back into her torn slipper. "Where you come from, anyway?"

"California. Berkeley, California. How long have you lived here?"

"All my life. Never been nowhere else. Did go to Little Rock once with my daddy, though."

Jubie wondered why Sachi didn't say nothing. Just looked away with wide eyes. Why was she so quiet all of a sudden? "Guess that was your mama in line with you?" She asked, trying to break the silence. "Where was your daddy?"

Sachi pointed to the stick Jubie still held. "What's that for?"

"Ah, nothing. I was just playing tic-tac-toe in the dirt." She tossed the stick aside. "So, your daddy ain't here?"

Sachi brushed her hair out of her face and took a deep breath. "Not here. Not anywhere."

At last, Jubie understood, and her eyes burned. "Oh. I get it. Sorry. My daddy's gone, too." She whispered so Sachi wouldn't hear her voice shake. "Been six months now. Happened just after Thanksgiving."

Sachi whispered. "My daddy–Papa–died the day after Christmas. . . a few days after some boys beat him up. All because he was Japanese." She picked at splinters on the fence post.

Now the sun scorched. Beads of sweat trickled down the sides of Jubie's face, and something swept her up in a dizzy swirl until she sank to the dirt. That image, the one she fought to keep pushed way back in dark corners of her mind, flashed up. Slapped her hard.

Daddy hanging from a tree. His eyes looking real sad. Mama screaming for someone to help her cut him down. The sound of his body when it hit the ground. The shock of his cold skin when she touched his hand.

It happened to Sachi's father, too? She'd never thought that kind of thing happened to other folk— happened in places other than Jerome. It was the reason she wanted to leave this place.

She blinked her eyes hard to chase away her tears. If only blinking hard would chase away that picture of Daddy. But it was burned in her memory like the brand on Lulu's hide.

Sachi moved closer to Jubie and blocked the sun, her shadow bringing cool relief. "You okay?"

Jubie looked up and smiled at Sachi. "Yeah, I'll be okay. Guess there ain't no other way to be." She picked up the stick she'd tossed aside and drew four crossed lines in the dirt. "Hey, let's play tic-tac-toe. You wanna be an X or O?"

Jan Morrill writes short stories and memoir essays. She has finished a novel and is currently trying to find a publisher. She graduated with a Bachelor of Arts Degree from Langston University. Her two children are grown and she now lives in Fayetteville, Arkansas with her husband. They enjoy their hobbies which include sailing and traveling.

A Love that Lasts
By Delois McGrew, Louella Turner
& Regina Williams

Rebecca's rocking chair creaked each time she toed it back and forth in front of the dying fire. At the thought of her son and husband, an occasional tear trickled down her thin cheek. Will had snuck away in the middle of the night to fight for the Confederacy. She begged him not to go. Her husband, Noah, told him he was too young, but Will had a mind of his own. Six months later, Noah set out, determined to bring Will home. She'd had no word from them since. Lately, she found herself staring into space for hours, and when she tried to recall their faces, they became fuzzy in her mind. When she couldn't remember them at all, would they cease to exist?

The morning sun bathed the treetops with light, turning them into a blaze of gold that reminded her of their first days on the farm. The rolling hills and rich forests that made Tennessee a place of wonder concealed the rock-rich soil she and Noah toiled to clear outside the small town of Chester. They settled on the property, not only for its beauty, but for its closeness to the village where they were born.

So many stones had been pulled from their one hundred acres, that a three-foot rock wall surrounded most of their land. It was a blessing their child hadn't been conceived until after the hard labor of clearing the ground was done. They named their son after Noah's father, William, and his father before him, and the scores of other Williams whose names were etched into the family Bible.

She shifted in her chair and sighed, her heart aching for Noah and Will. Her parents were long gone, and Noah's, too. Empty days and nights stretched behind her and the thought of a lonely future was more than she could bear. She felt her slight hold on sanity slipping as she tried to bring her son's face to mind.

Rebecca always knew her son would someday want more than the farm, but she hadn't expected it to be a war that would take him away. When word came that shots were fired on Fort Sumter, Will, along with all the other young men in the county, was eager to do his duty. He'd written them the day before the Battle of Shiloh saying he was thrilled to serve under General Pierre Gustav Beauregard against the Union forces of Ulysses S. Grant. After that bloody encounter, they received word he was missing.

The day after the news came, she watched Noah disappear down the road that ran in front of their cabin, shoulders straight, body leaning forward in the saddle, and it struck her how much the two men had grown alike. And how empty her life would be without them. She missed their times together, but especially the time they spent gathered around the table.

The evening meal had always been her favorite part of their day. She'd ring the dinner bell, then stand on the front porch while Will and Noah walked in from the fields, laughing and talking. Sometimes they seemed more like best friends than father and son. Then, in the soft glow of the kerosene lamp, she'd watch her men eat the food she lovingly prepared. At these moments, her life was complete.

Contentment also filled her when she and Noah lay spooned together in the large bed he made for her when they married. He worked for six months carving the intricate roses across the walnut headboard. Even after thirty years of marriage, it took only his touch to make her pulse race and her heart jump within her breast. This she missed most of all.

Today marked six months since Noah left, and still no word. She thought she would go crazy with worry before the day finally ended. That evening, she set the table with three plates, three knives, three forks, and three spoons. When she realized what she'd done, she quickly grabbed up the two extra plates. She stood there for a moment, silence echoing off the walls, then placed them carefully back, her husband's at the head of the table and Will's across from her. She could hear Reverend Wilkes scolding her for this folly. But he didn't have to sit at an empty table every night. When he tired of his own wife's cooking, he was always welcomed by the local widows, glad for a chance to cook for a man again.

That night, she avoided the bedroom until exhaustion finally drove her to the foot of her beautiful rose-carved bed. The emptiness of it overwhelmed her. At times—like now—her need for Noah filled her with desire, but she forced the feelings away. Like so many nights before, she spent this one in the rocking chair by the fireplace. While she drifted in and out of a restless sleep, tears of sorrow and desperation rolled down her pale cheeks. As always, her lips moved constantly in the half-prayer half-plea that came straight from her loving heart.

The next morning, a scuffling noise on the front porch brought her out of her uneasy sleep and to her feet. She'd dreamed of Noah. It had been so real the scent of his clean-shaven face still lingered in the air. She gave herself a shake and walked to the door. If the mayor or sheriff stood there, the news would probably be that one of her men was wounded or ill. But, God forbid, if Reverend Wilkes lurked on her front steps, then death itself would be at her hearth. Taking a deep breath, she forced herself to open the heavy pine door just an inch and peer out. It was only Widow Marcus. Rebecca opened the door and greeted the dour-faced woman draped in black.

"Heard any news yet?" the woman asked, pushing herself past Rebecca.

"No. But I will any day now."

"They're dead and you know it. They're all dead. All of them boys laying on the ground bloated up like dead sows. Horrible war. No sense to it. Men and their honor. Damn fools. Leavin' their crops to ruin, their women to fend for themselves." Widow Marcus stopped for a breath and eased her considerable bulk into the chair Rebecca pulled from the kitchen table.

"Got any water? I'm parched. Walked the whole way here. Them Blue Bellies took my last horse. Damn men." She took a large white handkerchief from her belt and fanned at her red face. Her glance skimmed over the three plates on the table, then she turned a curious eye toward Rebecca. "You had company?"

Rebecca's hand shook as she ignored the question and filled a dipper from the water bucket. Surely Widow Marcus couldn't be right. They couldn't be dead.

She reached for a cup from the drain board. It slipped from her grasp and crashed to the floor.

Shards of china skittered across the hard pine, and Widow Marcus flinched. "Sister Wilkes heard it from her husband who heard it from his cousin up near Nashville. He says there's dead boys in gray laying along the roads like cordwood."

Rebecca could bear the woman's voice no longer. "They're not dead," she said as she backed away from the widow. "Your man is dead. You buried him. But not mine. Noah and Will are alive. I know it." Anger flushed her cheeks, and she jerked the door open. "Now, get! I won't listen to any more of your lies."

Widow Marcus braced her hands against the table. The wood groaned as she pushed herself to her feet. "Ain't no sense gettin' fussy over it. I was just trying to help. It ain't good for you, living all alone way out here."

"Good day to you." Rebecca held the door wide.

In her haste to push her way out, the widow's black skirt caught on a nail. "People been sayin' you're teched in the head, and now I believe it. The Reverend Wilkes is gonna hear about this." She jerked her skirt free and lumbered down the steps.

Before the waddling figure was out of sight, Rebecca turned toward the kitchen. For an instant, Noah sat in his place at the head of the table smiling his approval. He'd always disliked the gossipy Widow Marcus.

With each passing hour, Noah and Will became more and more real to Rebecca. She chopped firewood with Noah looking over her shoulder. She mended Will's shirt while he watched. She ate supper with them at the table, the dim light softening their dear faces.

That night, while brushing her hair, Noah's reflection watched from the edge of their bed. The look in his eyes warmed her blood and reminded her of their wedding night. Slowly, she made her way across the room and sat on the lavender-scented bed covers. She laid back and her chestnut hair fanned out across the pillow. Hair the color of the gelding Noah rode away on. He told her he bought the high-priced animal because the color reminded him of her. Smiling, she curled her body into the familiar spooning position. When she felt the familiar weight of his arm encircle her waist, delight raced through her. She held her breath in wonder at what might follow.

Early the next morning, she watched the hunched form of Reverend Wilkes stomp across the unplowed field toward her cabin. The bottom of his scissor-tailed topcoat flapped in the wind, his head bent forward in determination. Widow Marcus hadn't wasted any time. Or was he here as a messenger of death? She considered not answering his knock, but when he pounded on the door a second time, she opened it and waited for him to speak.

"Sister Tucker," he said as he tried to see around her into the kitchen. "I just came by to see how you're doing. And to bring you the comfort of God's word."

"Thank you, but we don't need comforting. We're doing just fine."

Wilkes craned his neck to see past her. "We? Miz Tucker, are you telling me Noah has come home?"

Still barring his way, she turned her head and looked at the kitchen table, the three plates in their usual place. Her knees weakened and her head whirled. Had Noah come home? Or had last night only been a dream? Without a second's hesitation, and with no thought of the reverend and his offer of comfort, she slammed the door shut on his startled face.

Hurrying to the sanctuary of the bedroom, she closed the door behind her and leaned against it. She took in the bed, the rumpled coverlet, and the faint lingering scent of their love. Noah *had* held her in his arms last night. Afterwards, he'd kissed the soft hollow of her throat, whispered that their love was destined to last forever and he would always be with her. It *couldn't* have been a dream.

Two days later, Sissy Keeton found herself in the company of the Mrs. Reverend Wilkes and Widow Butler, trudging down the rutted dirt road toward the Tucker farm. Sissy hadn't wanted to come along, but Widow Butler and Mrs. Wilkes together made a formidable force. She cast an eye at the waning sun and hurried her pace to keep up with the other two, who walked as if their life depended on it.

"You know she isn't going to take to us showing up like this," said Widow Butler, grasping her walking stick harder and thrusting it into a patch of weeds in front of her like she was looking for snakes.

Mrs. Wilkes pursed her thin lips and stuck her sharp chin out further. "Don't matter. The reverend says it's better for us ladies to handle this."

"I'm not so sure about that." Sissy touched a hand to her tattered straw hat, tilting it to keep the setting sun from her face. "The poor soul's been through a lot. Like I told you before, she might see it as meddling." She knew she would. Why did she let them talk her into this?

"She's been through no more than the rest of us." Widow Butler dug her stick harder into the ground and propelled her girth along, her black skirt stirring up dust as she went. She gave Sissy a hard look over her shoulder. "We've both lost husbands. And you lost a son, too. We know what it's like."

Sissy flinched and felt the blood drain from her face. It was still hard to talk about her own double loss. "Rebecca has never been very strong," she said avoiding a pile of rocks from a fallen wall near the road. She lifted her skirt to keep it out of the dirt. She'd be glad when this sojourn was over.

"I'll agree to that. She's too soft." Widow Butler touched Sissy's arm and paused to rest.

Sissy waited, shading her eyes and looking at the sun drawing closer to the tree line with each passing moment.

"When I lost my Earl, I went on as if nothing had happened. Had to. Had a farm to run and four children to feed. No time to sit around and coddle myself. Rebecca just needs a good talking to."

"If only a talking to could fix it. I thought I couldn't live when I got word that Buddy died at Pea Ridge." Sissy's voice softened. "Then when my Jacob was killed only a month later, I *wanted* to die. I'd have done anything to bring them back. If I'd known what to do." She paused and her voice dropped to a whisper. "I'd have made a pact with the devil himself."

"What was that? You're mumbling again." Widow Butler leaned closer to Sissy.

She didn't respond, her eyes on Mrs. Wilkes, a short distance ahead, waiting in the middle of the road.

"Will the two of you stop chattering? We'd better get moving. Not one of us had the good sense to bring a lantern and I don't relish the idea of walking back in the pitch black."

Before Sissy could answer, Widow Butler spoke. "We are hurrying. We're just worried that because poor Rebecca is out here all alone she's lost her mind with grief."

Sissy loosened her collar and fanned herself with her hands. "Why, grief? None of us knows for sure her men ain't coming back. Maybe she's just lonely and doing things like setting the table with their plates as a kind of spell to bring them back. Or maybe it just makes her feel like they're all there together. That don't mean she's crazy."

"That's the dumbest thing I ever heard." Mrs. Wilkes planted her hands against her hips and glared at them. "The reverend says she's loony as can be. Said he saw the plates himself through the window. And she slammed the door right in his face. Good thing he's a forgiving man. Anyone else might have just left her to herself. But he says it's our duty to minister to such unfortunate souls." She turned to go on. "Now, can we get on before the night catches us?"

"It won't be that dark. It's to be a full moon tonight. I looked in the Almanac before we left. And, besides, we're almost there." Sissy pointed down the road. "I see the light in Rebecca's window."

When the Tucker cabin came into view, Sissy fell into line behind the other two, looking down at her feet and wishing she'd had enough courage to refuse this chore. When the single line of black skirts stopped, she bumped into Mrs. Wilkes, and looked up. Pale yellow light from a large window fanned itself out across the porch and the path leading to it.

"Go on up there and look in." Mrs. Wilkes propelled Sissy forward.

Widow Butler pushed her up the steps. "Make sure Rebecca's to home."

Sissy lifted her skirt and crept across the porch, constantly looking over her shoulder to make sure she hadn't been deserted. When she reached the window, she placed her face near the bubbled glass. She stood stock-still for a second, amazed at what she saw, then turned with fingers pressed to her lips.

"What's the matter?" Widow Butler whisper sounded loud in the stillness of the twilight. "Your eyes are round as that moon up there."

Sissy hurried down the stairs, nearly tripping on her petticoat. She held her hands to her breast and leaned forward to catch her breath. "There's three people in there," she said. "Couldn't see them clear, but I'd swear one of them is Will."

The two women stared at her, then up at the window.

Mrs. Wilkes broke the silence. "Well, that's wonderful," she gushed. "Don't you see? He's come home safe and sound. And maybe Noah's in there, too. Let's go welcome them home." She started toward the porch.

"No, wait," Widow Butler grabbed her arm. "There's something wrong here. Let's all take a look first."

Sissy moved forward reluctantly, only to find herself in the lead, with Widow Butler and Mrs. Wilkes clinging to her. When she arrived at the window, Sissy placed her face up to the edge of the pine window frame as before and the other two women followed her. Good thing no one was around. They must look like three old crows, one head atop the other, all in black and packed together like this.

After one quick glance, Sissy felt herself being pulled away from the window and back down the steps.

"I swear they were there when I looked before." Sissy said to the two women. "There were two men at that table and one of them was Will."

"Well, they ain't there now," Widow Butler whispered. "Where could they have gone so fast? There's something fishy goin' on here, and I aim to get to the bottom of it right now." She stomped to the door loud as she could and rapped her meaty knuckles against it.

When the latch clicked, Mrs. Wilkes took a step back and Sissy heard her praying under her breath.

Light from the cabin stretched itself across the porch when Rebecca opened the door, a quizzical expression on her face. She looked at Widow Butler and the other two, then over her shoulder at the kitchen table. Finally, she turned back to the woman at the door.

"What a surprise," she said, nodding to each of them in turn. "Widow Butler, Widow Keeton, Mrs. Wilkes. Isn't it rather late for you ladies to be out this far?"

"The reverend sent us," Widow Butler said firmly. "We're all worried about you. May we come in?"

Rebecca looked over her shoulder again, then moved aside and made a welcoming gesture. "Well, since you're here, I guess it wouldn't be neighborly to not invite you in. But I assure you I'm fine. There's no need for worry."

Once inside, Sissy glanced around the long narrow room with the kitchen at the far end. Did the other two feel as foolish as she did? The table set for three caught her attention, then she shifted her eyes back to Rebecca. She saw the other women looking at the table, too.

"Why, I do declare. If you don't look just grand." Mrs. Wilkes cocked her head and looked Rebecca up and down. "You're fairly blooming. I thought from what my husband said you'd be . . ." She faltered, then fell silent.

Widow Butler took it up. ". . . crazy with grief."

A faint smile played across Rebecca's lips. "I'm sure you did. Well, now that you've seen that I'm fine, you can tell Reverend Wilkes he doesn't have to worry about me anymore."

Sissy could see that Widow Butler wasn't going to be that easily satisfied.

"Just a minute. If you're so fine, why do you have three place settings at the table?"

"Why shouldn't I? If it makes me feel better to set places for my Noah and Will, then what's the harm in that?"

Sissy didn't think there was any harm in it, and looking into the eyes of the other women, it appeared they felt the same. But she was curious about one thing. "Rebecca, I peeped in the window just before we knocked and I thought . . . well, I thought I saw someone else at the table with you."

Rebecca's gaze never wavered as she looked into the face of each of her visitors, then back at Sissy. "Who would that be?"

"Uh. It appeared to be two men, and one of them looked like your Will."

"That's a poor jest to play. I expect Will and Noah will be coming home soon, but you don't see them around here right now, do you?"

"Oh, my, no, I didn't intend it as a jest. I'm so sorry. I guess . . . I guess my eyes were playing tricks on me." Sissy twisted her hands together, and wished she'd stayed home.

"That's all right." Rebecca smiled at her. "These are hard times for everyone."

Rebecca's kind words pierced Sissy's gentle heart. It was time for them to leave this woman in peace. She turned toward her fellow travelers, and in doing so, looked once more at the kitchen table. Something out of the ordinary there made her anxious to remove herself and her companions at once.

"We've bothered Rebecca enough. It's time we got ourselves home. Plenty of dirt to sweep off our own doorsteps." Before they could protest, she had them hustled out of the cabin ahead of her.

While they made their way across the porch, exclaiming over the lateness of the hour, Sissy turned back to where Rebecca stood, outlined by the light spilling out from behind her. She kept her voice low. "Many's the time I wished to see my man and son again. I reckon if you knew how I could do that, you'd tell me, wouldn't you?"

The figure in the door hesitated before answering. "I wish I could. Sometimes, wonders occur, and we don't know why or how. When it happens, it's not ours to question, but to just hold it close, because we don't know how long it will last." With that, she stepped back and closed the door.

Sissy threw a hurried glance after the two dark silhouettes scurrying down the moonlit dirt road, then hesitated. After a bit, she turned and looked through the kitchen window for a long moment. Nodding her head in satisfaction, she continued down the steps and followed the other two, who were headed toward home like barn-sour horses. So that's why there had been half-eaten food on all three plates. My eyes weren't playing tricks on me, after all.

Back inside the Tucker cabin, the meal was finished, the kitchen tidied, and lamps blown out. The only light came from a flickering candle on the walnut dresser facing the rose-carved bed. Rebecca gave one last brush stroke to her long hair, and gazed into the reflection of Noah's deep blue eyes. When his arms reached for her, she bent her head and blew out the candle. He'd kept his word—that their love was to last forever and he would always be with her. For now, that was enough.

An award winning writer, Delois McGrew is published in fiction, non-fiction and poetry. Her publishing credits include national magazines and regional newspapers, as well as several short story anthologies. While her cozy mystery series searches for a publisher, she is at work on a paranormal romance.

Delois has edited or co-edited six short story anthologies; Echoes of the Ozarks, Voices, and Skipping Stones.

Concentrating on her writing since 2003 when she moved to Springdale, Arkansas, Delois joined the Northwest Arkansas Writers Workshop and is also a member of Ozarks Writers League, where she has served as Director, Treasurer, Newsletter Editor, and currently serves as President.

#

Louella Turner lives in St. Charles, MO with her husband, mother, youngest son, two dogs and the cat from hell. She writes, serves on the board of several writing groups, teaches fiction and helps run High Hill Press, a retirement venture. She has published nearly 100 short stories and essays, and won that many awards

for her work. Her latest novel is about a family of Holy Roller vampire and demon slayers, and although her family is very much like the family in the book, she claims her characters are completely fictional.

Regina Williams has had stories published in *Future's Mysterious Anthology Magazine*, *Midwest Literary Review* and *Shorelines Literary Review*, to name a few. She is an award-winning author and has a novel making the rounds at the publishing houses. Regina is also the editor of *The Storyteller*.

The Fate of Tate
By Brenda Brinkley

*J*asper Tate lay dead as an armadillo trying to cross the road during rush hour. Becky should scream, or faint, or do something girly. Instead, she burst into laughter. The contemptible coot was long overdue for some good, old-fashioned justice, and somebody had delivered it. But who? The laughter stopped.

If she called the police, there would be an investigation. Inquiries would bring all kinds of ugly details to light. Friendships would be trashed. Families shattered. Ashamed of her relief, a tear trickled down her cheek. How had she ever allowed herself to fall for him? How could someone so mean be so charming? Ten years ago, at the ripe old age of nineteen, she became another notch on his bedpost, and had kicked herself ever since.

With jobs in short supply, Becky swallowed her pride and became a waitress at the T-Bone Café. A ridiculous name since there wasn't a t-bone on the menu.

Becky looked into the face of her boss, and for the first time did not feel intimidated. The blue eyes that once pierced her heart now stared, cold and blank, at the ceiling. He might be looking up, but unless he had a last-minute change of heart, his final destination was far from heavenly.

She grabbed a nearby tablecloth and draped it over his head. The man didn't scare her, but the dead body was a different story. A chill crept up her spine as the reality of the situation sank in. She shivered.

Startled by the ring of the telephone, Becky stepped backward and bumped into a table. Good heavens! As jittery as a cat with eight expired lives, she let the phone ring. Jasper couldn't force her to open the cafe today, or any other day. She inched toward the door and locked it. A sign. She needed to put a sign on the door. Everyone in town knew Jasper would never stand for his business to be closed. You can't make money that way. She looked at the tablecloth on the floor. He would never squeeze another dime out of anybody in this town, or any other.

CLOSED FOR INVENTORY. She taped the sign to the front door. No one would question that Jasper wanted to keep track of his assets. With the blinds closed, Becky removed the phone from its holder.

"Danny, is Leon there?" She hated to drag anyone into this mess, but she trusted her brothers. "I need the two of you to come to the cafe. Come around to the back door. I'll explain when you get here."

Not wanting to answer any questions, she didn't wait for a response. Becky clicked the Off button.

Voices indicated the coffee crowd was gathering and none too happy about the locked door. "Nobody said a thing about any inventory."

She recognized Willie Hawkins's voice. It was hard to believe Willie still patronized the cafe owned by the man who devised the nastiest smear campaign in the history of Glory, Missouri. Jasper didn't want to be mayor, but he made sure Willie's brother, Ben, didn't get the job. He wanted a "yes" man in the position and never gave a thought to the havoc he created while making it happen. It was also a well-known fact, Jasper wanted Ben's wife. Connie Hawkins turned him down flat, and with injured pride, he retaliated.

Rumors started without a shred of proof to back them up. Ben's wife endured all she could. She divorced him and left town with their three children. The rumors proved to be false, but not before Ben lost his wife, kids, and the election. Yes, Becky reasoned, Ben had plenty of reasons to want Jasper dead.

Karen! Becky's fingers trembled as she punched numbers on her cell phone. Please let her be running late, as usual.

"Hello."

"Karen, it's Becky." She had to make sure the cook didn't show up for work.

"Hey, I'm sorry I'm late. Is your stomach acting up again?"

"No, I'm fine." Becky blushed. "But Jasper isn't up to opening the cafe today, so we've got the day off."

"What's wrong? That tightwad would have to be at death's door not to open for business."

He wasn't at death's door, he'd gone through it. "I didn't ask any questions," Becky said. "Just glad for the day off." Positive her voice didn't sound as carefree as she wanted, Becky ended the conversation.

"Hey, sis, what's going on?"

She heaved a sigh of relief at the sound of her brother's voice. "I'm in here, Leon."

"What the devil's going on? I was fixing to work on my Mustang." Her older brother loved to tinker with cars, but that was the extent of his exertion. He would never be labeled a workaholic.

She pointed at the floor.

"When did you start covering the floor with tablecloths?"

"Jasper is under it."

"Well, that's dumb. What's he doing under there?"

"He's dead, Leon. Someone killed him."

"Who would want to do that?" Danny, her younger brother, stared at the covered lump on the floor.

Leon laughed. "Who wouldn't? Ain't a person in the county that'll miss him. His grandma, bless her sweet soul, was the only one who could tolerate him."

Jasper's grandmother raised him after the death of his parents in a car crash. A huge insurance settlement was placed in a trust fund until he was twenty-one. Becky watched, with the rest of the town, as his grandmother spoiled him. Nobody blamed her. It was a natural response to a tragic situation. But as Jasper grew older, he grew mean. He had money. He knew it, and he knew how to use it, but not in a good way.

Shock filled the town when Jasper's grandmother put the deed of her home in his name and he evicted her. She lasted one month at Pleasant Villa Senior Living Facility. Everyone believed her death was the result of a broken heart.

"I guess you'd better call the sheriff," Danny mumbled.

"I can't call Roy. He would have to arrest somebody." Becky's voice shook.

"Yeah, that's what happens when somebody gets killed."

"But do we really want one of our friends to go to jail for getting rid of the trash?"

"You can't just leave him there." Danny plopped into the nearest chair, removed his cap, and scratched his head.

"Why do you think I called you? I can't move him by myself."

"Where are we going to take him?" Danny scratched his scalp harder.

"Quit raking your head like you've got fleas," Becky scolded. "We've got to bury him where nobody will ever find him."

"Bury him?" Leon took a step backward. "People will start asking questions. He'll be missed."

"Folks may wonder where he's gone, but like you said, he won't be missed." Becky hoped her brothers would soon discover their backbones. "If his funeral was held tomorrow, mourners would have to be hired."

"But a person can't just disappear," Danny protested.

"Jimmy Hoffa did," Becky asserted.

"Jimmy's missing?" Danny's eyes widened. "I just saw him yesterday at the hardware store."

"That was Jimmy Hoefner, not Hoffa." Leon slapped his forehead.

Becky wanted to slap them both. "We can't stand around all day. Let's get rid of this body." She stooped and removed the tablecloth.

"You said he was murdered," Leon said. "Where's the blood?"

The shock of discovering Jasper's dead body caused Becky to leap to, what she considered, the obvious conclusion.

"Maybe he had a heart attack," Leon offered.

"You'd have to have a heart first," Becky scoffed.

"He didn't have a heart?" Nobody would ever mistake Danny for a Rhodes Scholar. "You can't live without a heart."

Leon cackled. "He's dead, ain't he?"

"Maybe somebody suffocated him with a pillow," Danny said. "I've seen that on TV."

"Well, on TV did the guy lie down on the floor so they could kill him?" Leon slapped his knee and laughed harder.

"He could've been taking a nap." Danny's face turned red.

"Jasper Tate taking a nap on the floor. I guess he was using the tablecloth as a blanket."

Her younger brother shrugged. "You explain it then."

First-hand knowledge told Becky that Jasper wasn't above rolling around on the floor, but napping there was a different story. Fed up with the dimwitted duo, she snapped, "We don't have time to explain it. We've got to get him out of here." If they didn't get a move on, they were going to be caught with a dead body and no explanation. "We'll take him out the back door. Leon, get behind him and lift."

"I ain't ever touched a dead body," her brother hesitated. "Well, I do throw out dead mice for momma. But that's different."

"A varmint is a varmint. Now come on," Becky urged.

Leon stepped behind Jasper's head and bent down. "I'm gonna sit him up. You grab his arms and hold him steady till I get a good hold of him around the chest."

Danny moaned.

Beads of sweat formed on Leon's brow as he raised the dead man to a sitting position.

"Hurry up. I'm gonna be sick." With a firm grip on Jasper's arms, Danny stood straddling the lower part of the corpse.

"Nobody's going to be sick," Becky ordered.

"Not even you? You've been looking puny lately."

Exasperated that Leon had chosen this particular time to become observant, she insisted, "I'm fine. Now get him out of here."

Taking a deep breath, Leon put his arms around Jasper's chest, clasped his hands together, and lifted.

"Wait!"

Startled, Leon relaxed his hold. "Do you want him out of here or not?"

"Look." Becky pointed at something on the floor.

"A peanut. So what?"

"It just popped out of Jasper's mouth. That fool choked to death on a peanut."

"Nobody killed him?" Danny was as pale as the corpse.

"Nobody killed him."

"Can we call the police now, sis?" Relief flooded Leon's face.

"Yep. We'll let the police take care of this mess," Becky answered.

"Hallelujah! We were doing a terrible job."

Becky picked up the telephone and looked at the lifeless body on the floor. She took a deep breath and exhaled. Alive or dead, Jasper Tate was trouble.

Her hand came to rest on her stomach. She knew better than to drink, but Jasper offered her a beer. One led to two. Add Willie Nelson on the radio, and they were on the road again, so to speak. One stupid night, a few short weeks ago, changed her life forever.

Her fear of fighting him for custody ended with his life. No one knew, and no one would. Her baby deserved better.

Brenda Brinkley has had over 300 articles published in magazines and newspapers. She has won awards for her fiction writing at conferences throughout the midwest. She's also had short stories in a variety of publications, including Echoes of the Ozarks, Voices, Cuivre River, and Writing on Walls anthologies. Also an award winning photographer, Brenda's work has been used on magazine and anthology covers.

Born and raised in the Ozarks, Brenda lives on a farm in Webster County with her husband, Gary. They will celebrate their 36th anniversary this year. They have two grown children and five delightful grandchildren. When she isn't writing, she loves to read, grow and decorate gourds, and weave rugs on her grandmother's loom.

The Sound of Death
Erin York

As the snow outside my window melts, I squint my eyes.

That mirror there is dreadful. It sits across from my bed and my reflection stares at me all through the night. This morning, the thing with grey hair and grey skin that I've become, looks far from rested.

The whistling snore beside me stops.

Fear pushing self-pity away, I whirl around.

"Fin? Fin!" I touch his bony shoulder with shaking fingers. "Fin!"

He looks pained, lying there with wrinkles upon wrinkles criss-crossing over his face. I don't want him to die, not yet, not here. I'm not ready. I still love him as much as I did 65 years ago on our wedding day.

Crying, I nudge him again. He always was a sound sleeper.

"Wha—huh? I—" Fin opens his eyes. "Georgia, you're crying. What's wrong? Are you all right?"

Slowly, he raises his elbow while I replay every last word the doctors said just days ago.

His heart...we don't know how long it'll hold up. He's 83 and been through a lot.

They always whisper about death. I don't understand why.

"Nothing," I pat his hand, "it's nothing. I'm sorry I woke you."

He yawns and glances at his watch. "It's getting late. I think I'll hop in the shower."

I nod, "Good idea. You take a long hot shower while I run to the post office. When I come back, we can eat."

He gives me this look that's almost angry.

"Why don't you wait to run errands, then I can go with you?"

I heave an inward sigh, "The doctors told you to take it easy. It'll take me five minutes. I'll be back before you know it."

Fin wants to argue, I can see it in his eyes, but he doesn't. Instead, he utters a grunt and throws the blankets back. The sheet catches on his left foot, his bad side. He struggles to reach his hand down his body. He's shaking with exertion, wheezing, a frail man who I can't save.

I want to help him, but I know better than to even try. At last, he's free.

He stands and hobbles away from me. The cold has stiffened his body so much it hurts for me to watch him walk. Right now, I despise winter, the season that once was my favorite.

Fin throws on his robe and opens our bedroom door.

"Fin…"

He stops.

"I love you."

He turns and manages a smile, "I love you too."

Then, he's out of my sight, and I'm alone. I realize I've been clenching my hands so tightly the skin is indented with deep crescent moons.

"I love you," I whisper. "I love you."

I have never felt so alone as now. Why does it feel that though my Fin still breathes and speaks, he's already dead?

I dress warmly and quickly, then hurry out of our bedroom. I stop by the bathroom and peek in.

Fin's still dressed.

"I'm leaving."

He looks at me through empty eyes, "Goodbye."

"I love you."

This time he doesn't say it back.

I close the door behind myself. In my head, I reassure myself that he does love me. He's just scared, just lost in thought. I run my fingers over the wooden bathroom door that separates us. It's cold, hard, unbendable, just like the death doctors whisper about.

Can I let go of him? No, that's why I'm so cold.

The house, the world, everything is grey like my aging skin. Where is the color? Where are the rainbows and romantic sunsets? Those 63 years are only a second past, but yet an eternity ago.

As I stand there, convincing myself to let go of the doorknob, I hate time. If time would only stop, then everything would be all right. I don't want my husband to leave me alone.

Somehow I tear myself from the bathroom door. It hurts to walk, but the pain is not physical, not mental. Instead, it's something so deep, it's beyond human understanding. I pause and think a lot has been beyond my understanding lately.

I unlatch the screen door, and a blast of freezing air slams into me. I lose my grip on the door and the howling wind rushes around me, desperate to outdo the heater.

"No!" I shout as I fight to keep the warmth, the life, inside the house.

The cold surrounds me, makes my nose and my eyes threaten to leak. Determined not to let the weather get the best of me, I pull up my hood and wade through it.

My car is a beacon.

I start the engine and huddle with only my body heat until it begins to warm. At least, I scraped the ice off yesterday; I don't have the energy to do it today.

I back out of my driveway, staring at the dark, empty house I'm supposed to call home. No lights are on; no candles are lit. It looks like I already live alone

Being out is good for me. The radio kicks on half-way through the drive, and I listen to Billy Joel. After dropping off the mail, mostly bills, I begin to feel hungry. I'll fix scrambled eggs with extra butter and toast from the loaf I made a couple of days ago. Fin and I can pretend we are twenty years younger again. I smile.

I open the front door. The house still feels cold. "Fin?"

He's not sitting in his chair like he normally does. I check my watch. I'd been gone longer than I expected; the roads were icy.

The shower's still on.

I let out my breath, glad for something other than silence.

"Fin?"

I drop off the car keys and my heavy winter coat in our bedroom. He doesn't answer, so I shrug and walk to the bathroom door.

I knock before opening it. The curtain is pulled tightly around the shower. It smells, and I wish for the millionth time Fin would flush the toilet before he gets in the shower.

"I'm back. How about eggs and toast for breakfast?" What do you want to drink?"

I tap my fingers on the sink as I wait for a reply, but there isn't one. My heart beats faster, too fast. Why can't I hear him in the shower? All I hear is water, pounding water, just—just water.

"Fin." My voice sounds like I'm choking on air. I'm terrified to pull back the curtain. "Fin."

My legs start moving and I can't stop them. I throw open the curtain, wishing I could step back, close my eyes, wishing I could do something to—

"No."

I cover my mouth, bite down on my fingers. Burning pain shoots through my chest. I cannot breathe. I cannot *breathe*.

He's crumpled on the bathtub floor. One hand is pressed to his chest. I can't see his face, only grey hair soaked through. I can't see his face, but I can imagine it. He's not moving, not breathing.

He twitches, and it's an involuntary spasm that streaks through his right side. His body slumps to the side, and I see brownish streaks running along the grooves in the bathtub. That's where the smell was coming from.

Suddenly, my breath rushes from my lungs in realization. My husband, my Fin, my love, is dead.

The room spins, starts to focus, then spins again. I clutch the sink, trying not to gag. I look back at Fin.

He's so naked, so exposed, lifeless. The shell of his body seems so small, no longer protective and strong. He's left me alone.

The smell is too much. I lean over the sink and throw up stomach acid until my throat feels ragged.

I stumble from the bathroom, towards a phone. I want to pick it up; I want to dial the number for help, but I'm not sure if I can speak. I stare at the phone, trying to remember how to dial a number.

9. 1. 1. Each number takes an eternity to press.

"Hello? Yes, my husband, my Fin, he—he's dead. He's dead, and he's in the shower, and I haven't even turned off the—My address? 1309 Belton Street. It's the house with brick—Wait, I—"

The phone cuts off. They're sending someone over, but I didn't even—

My train of thought breaks.

I get to my feet and almost run back to the bathroom. This time, I don't notice the stench. I turn off the water and kneel by Fin's body. I touch his shoulder; it's cold and spongy, not hard like I expected.

I reach for a towel and run it over him.

"I love you." My voice cracks as I cradle the back of his head. "I love you."

I'm sobbing so hard my knees hit the porcelain tub with every heave of breath. I pull him into my laps, heedless of the saliva from his mouth on my arm and of his wet skin on my winter clothes.

"I love you and you left me."

Agony laces into my bones.

"You didn't wait until I got back to say good-bye."

I shake him.

"Why couldn't' you wait?"

He doesn't reply, doesn't acknowledge me. Of course he doesn't; he's dead. But he can't be dead! He can't; I love him!

"Say it." I squeeze his lips. His eyes are open, staring, but his beautiful grey irises have rolled back in his head. He can't see me, hear me, feel me. "Say you love me!"

The doorbell rings.

I jolt, let his body go, and stand. His blank face is tilted towards me. His image is one of a perverse child, mutilated with age. I shudder.

I love Fin, but I hate this corpse, this *thing,* he left behind.

I leave it behind and walk to the front door.

"Ms. Georgia Couch?"

"Mrs.," I say coldly. "Come in."

I look at the men in orange, blue, and white uniforms, and I resent their life, their youth. They have no right to put color in my grey world.

"Can you take us to him?"

I nod and lead them into my home. They walk into the bathroom, and I can't bear to go in after them.

I listen to them whisper and jostle things around.

I feel ghostly, inhuman. All I want is for this to be a dream, a doctor's whisper about death, but that's too much to ask this time. As the uniformed men take Fin and our 65 years of marriage, death is not whispering, but screaming all around me.

Erin York is a 19-year-old writer from the outskirts of Kansas City, Missouri, pursuing her undergraduate in Communications. She is editor of *Shorelines Literary Magazine*. Look for her work in *The Rogue Poetry Review, Chanterelle's Notebook, Beanery Press*, and other online and in print presses. Visit her website at: www.pushbuttonmuse.jimdo.com.

Justice
By Duke Pennell

*O*t was the first of May. After a dismal winter, spring brought cherry blossoms and warm sunshine to Washington . . . and I hated it. While life ran rampant out there, I was stuck in the office, dying.

My secretary, Susan Conway, peeked through the open doorway. "Justice Maslow, that reporter is here to see you."

The motherly type, Susan used every excuse to check up on me, even though I was old enough to be her father. A sweet little gal, but exasperating—like most women.

"Send him in, Susan."

A vision of loveliness strode briskly through the doorway and up to my desk, her hand outreached to shake mine. "Will I do instead, sir?" she asked. Her mouth smiled, but the arch of her eyebrows telegraphed her aggressiveness. "Julie Wilson, Your Honor."

I stood, took her hand, and looked her over. The beauty pageant type—trim, in her late twenties or early thirties, professionally groomed and well dressed. Blonde, sexy, and with a firm grip.

Pushy, spoiled little bitch.

"Miss Wilson. Please have a seat." I released her hand and motioned to a chair. "What can I do for you?"

"I want to get your story." She ticked off my vital statistics. "George Thomas Maslow, age seventy-four, Associate Justice of the Supreme Court, widower. A Rich Old White Man." The corner of her mouth turned up in a smirk. "I think you're—"

A flash of pain swept through my left leg. Balled my fists and clenched my teeth. "Miss Wilson, I don't have time for this. My background is well-documented. Nothing of import has occurred since I joined this court, over twenty years ago. What are you after?"

She locked her gaze with mine for a few seconds. "All right, let's cut to the chase. You have advanced bone cancer. Terminal osteosarcoma. Yet, you haven't stepped down from the bench. Why not?"

"How I deal with my illness is *my* business, young lady, not yours." I bit off the words. "If that's all you want to talk about, you can leave now."

She plowed ahead. "Then let's talk about Professor Patel at MIT. Nanotechnology and nerve cells. Does that ring any bells for you?"

She knows. Can't have any interference now, we're too close.

"MIT? Miss Wilson, if you had done your homework, you would know I set up a scholarship there, in my late wife's name." I rubbed my aching left leg. "I really am hard-pressed to see why any of this is of interest to you."

I tapped the override button on the morphine pump under my shirt. The last couple of months, the contraption had become my best friend, the steady drizzle of narcotic keeping my pain under control, but I needed more now. I hit the button again.

Christ, let it work soon!

"Are you all right?" She frowned. "You don't look so good."

The pain became a fire inside my leg, raging higher and higher. It wrenched me into a ball and I slumped out of the chair to the floor, arms locked around my left knee,

knee pulled tight to my chest. Through jaws gritted shut, I said, "Get Susan!"

She bolted to the door. "Miss Conway! Help!"

In seconds, Susan knelt by me. "Sir! What is it?"

My breath hissed out. "Call Dr. Williams at Georgetown. Tell him I said, 'It's got to be now.'" I hit the override button again and again and again, until it brought darkness and oblivion.

I came to on a hard hospital gurney. The pain was worse than ever, and it was all I could do to keep from screaming.

Dr. Williams looked down at me and frowned. "Maslow, are you sure about this?"

"Jesus Christ, Williams! What choice do I have?"

"None that I can see. I doubt you'll live through the night."

I was tired, tired of the fight and tired of the agony. "Just get on with it."

He looked around to his team, nodded, and said, "All right. Let's begin."

A nurse injected something into an IV line, and a soft, warm cloud enveloped me.

God, it doesn't hurt anymore. Dying will be worth it.

I floated away, into the blackness.

Staring at my own dead body, I thought how *odd* it is to outlive yourself.

My vision didn't work well—sharp, then blurred, then sharp again—like a camera focused by an inept photographer. My body lay on an operating table to my left, with Dr. Williams by its head. Half-a-dozen people in dull red scrubs moved about the room. The smell of disinfectant overrode the cloying, sweet odor of blood.

It wasn't a very attractive body—old, worn, and emaciated from the ravages of cancer.

Looks like a cadaver. Hell, it is a cadaver, and the cadaver is me. No, it only used to be me. Good God, this will take some getting used to. A brain transplant! Who'd have believed it? The doctors and engineers really outdid themselves this time. I'm alive and not insane. I hope!

A wave of relief and disbelief at my survival—against all odds—overwhelmed me and spilled out in a peal of girlish laughter. The sound shocked me into silence. I looked down at my new body, saw beneath the sheet the unmistakable shape of two feminine breasts.

What the . . . !

My gaze sought out Dr. Williams.

"I'm a *woman*?"

And everything went black.

The nurses tell me I was unconscious for two days. Something about psychic shock. What an understatement! I still seethed over the unforgiveable wrongness of it when Dr. Williams paid me a visit.

"What the hell did you do to me?"

Dr. Williams wore a perplexed expression. "Maslow, you knew going into this that nothing was certain—not the least of which was you simply living through it. You ought to be pleased to be alive, not complaining about the *vehicle* of your survival."

I sat on the edge of the bed in my hospital suite, attendants on each side of me, catching me whenever my balance failed. My legs dangled over the side. My young legs. My young slim legs. My young slim legs the rich brown color of mocha latte. I shook my head in dismay.

"Williamsh,"—my voice was high-pitched, almost soprano, and slurred, like some intoxicated teenybopper—"we agreed we were to use the body of that middle-aged man, that Michaels. He and I were from the same ethnic makeup and there would be fewer political repercussions. Not to mention, we were both mature males! Now, I am thrust into this . . . this black girl-child's body? Why, sir? Damn you, why? My entire life has been spent attaining a certain level of respect and confidence from my peers. You have taken all that away from me. *Death* would have been preferable!"

Williams's tone was matter-of-fact. "Unfortunately, there was a mechanical breakdown in the blood oxygenation unit that kept the Michaels body viable. Cellular decomposition set in."

"But this?" I indicated my body with a jerky sweep of my hand. "You couldn't have chosen more poorly!"

"We *had* no choice. You and your donor body have AB negative blood, something you share with only one percent of the population. Also, her cause of death was an inoperable cranial aneurysm, with no physical damage to anything but her brain. You were extraordinarily lucky."

"The surgery was successful? Then why am I mangling my speech? Why am I not in control of this body?"

He shook his head. "We don't know. The surgery went well, better than we'd hoped. The nanites connected the nerves from your brain to the appropriate nerves in the body. The autonomic and gross motor signals are getting through to the muscles, but not the fine controls. We believe as you use the muscles more, your brain will come to recognize the feedback it gets and will re-learn the control sequences. In essence, you're driving a car that's strange to you. Once you get used to it, everything will be fine."

"*Everything will be fine,*" I sneered. "You have no idea what you're talking about. The drugs you've given me will wear off soon and this euphoria along with them."

Dr. Williams looked at me curiously. "I believe you're operating under a misconception. You're not in pain. 'Euphoria,' you called it?"

"Yes. It's wonderful. But I can't stay on narcotics forever."

"You aren't on any. The euphoria you feel? That's the normal state for the body you have now." He grinned. "Get used to it."

"No drugs?" I was thunderstruck. *No more pain?* "But," I fretted, ". . . but what about these tubes you have stuck in me?"

"Just a saline drip and a catheter. We'll take them out in a day or so. Maslow, we'll keep you here for a while, to be certain there are no problems, but I'm confident all you need is some physical therapy to help you adjust to your new body." He sent me a considering look. "You ought to be thankful. Your whole life is ahead of you—again."

Physical therapy began the next day. Two burly male nurse aides came to accompany me, and I railed against being treated like an invalid. I slurred, "I'm a seventy-four-year old man, for God's sake! I know how to walk!" The fact that I still sounded like a drunken twit irritated me even more.

That attitude lasted until I stood up. Then a bird flew by my window, catching my attention—and the aides caught me as I fell. The legs worked as long as I consciously exercised control, but when I no longer thought about it, they quit.

Embarrassed, I stood again. This time, I thought only about walking. At each step I had to maintain my balance—front to rear, side to side—while I remembered where the last foot was and decided where the next foot should go, never forgetting to keep tension in the supporting leg while drawing the unsupported leg forward. Consciously, without fail. Because any time my concentration flagged, down I went.

So, flanked by my keepers, I jolted and swayed for the better part of an hour along the hallway from my room to the elevator and back. Finally, they helped me back into bed, pulled up the rails, and left.

As they walked out of my room, one said to his partner, "Didja hear her say she was a seventy-four year old man? Ha! Cutest old man *I've* seen in a while."

And there it was. I wasn't me anymore. No matter how much better this body was than my old one, I had lost myself. I had *become* a young black woman.

It took a few weeks, but I began to adjust. I was even able to look at this new body with some objectivity. She might have been a dancer because I had a very nice figure, well-rounded, the kind that would have excited me in my old life. Exploring it was different and, well, fun—I sort of lusted after it. And I slowly learned to cope. Even so, there were rude awakenings of several varieties in store. For instance, the first time someone made a pass at me.

I'd found swimming was great physical therapy, helping me become accustomed to my new body and keeping it in good tone at the same time. One afternoon, about three weeks into my therapy, there was a break in the routine. The regular aide, John, wasn't at the hospital pool. An attendant I hadn't seen before watched as I exercised. I was doing a backstroke when hands touched my shoulders and back and I looked up to see the new guy's tan, thirty-something face. "Thanks, but I'm fine. I don't need you."

"Sure you do, baby." His voice was soft, with the tone you use to calm a skittish kitten. The hand glided over my back, stopped under my rear end and gave a slight squeeze. "You need what I've got . . . and you know it."

"Get your hands off me!" I thrashed in the water to an upright position, but his hand stayed on my butt.

"Now, baby, don't be like that. You know this is what you want." He pulled me toward him, his other hand reaching up for my breasts.

I was frantic. What do you do when NO doesn't work? Slug him? I didn't know! I drew back my fist just as the regular attendant showed up.

"What's going on here? *Leave her alone!*" John bellowed from the entry door.

Free, I thrashed through the water to the side, jerked myself out of the pool, and stood trembling—not in fear—in rage.

With a peremptory motion of his arm, John banished my erstwhile "aide" from the pool area then came to my side. "Are you okay? He didn't hurt you, did he?"

Physically, I was unharmed, but I remembered the many times I'd heard some young woman complain about a guy being "all hands." I'd always chalked it up to the girl getting what she'd asked for, but I hadn't invited that jerk's attentions in any way. I found my long-held attitudes were running into the wall of a new reality. It was a most disconcerting feeling.

The day before I left the hospital, I met with Dr. Williams again.

"Williams, who am I? George or Georgia? Don't misunderstand, my memories are perfectly intact and I know who I was. But since inhabiting this body, my mood seems to change more easily. That's what a Georgia would do. I understand it's because of different hormones and all that, but . . . what's to become of me? Am I to be a man, trapped in a woman's body? A woman? What?"

"Only time will tell, but you might want to change your name to the feminine version. With your appearance, it could make things easier. The videos of the surgery and our affidavits can document who you are, but after that— you're just going to have to find your own way. I imagine you'll face some interesting challenges."

He didn't know the half of it.

Spring had come again to D.C., and new life bloomed everywhere. I sat in my office and reveled in the day. Another May first—my new birthday—my fifth. A friend and I were on for our annual celebratory lunch and I was particularly anxious.

"Justice Maslow, that reporter is here to see you."

"Thank you, Susan. I'm going to take the rest of the day off. Why don't you do the same? You work too hard."

A striking young woman strode through the doorway, a million-dollar smile on her face. "Justice Maslow. You're looking good."

"Julie! You're early." She looked as gorgeous as she had five years ago, a radiant blonde with a fabulous face and figure.

"The firstest with the mostest, that's me. How's life treating you, now that you're a setter instead of a pointer? Had any more new insights since the last time we talked?" She sat on the couch next to the window and crossed those beautiful legs.

I went to a sideboard, opened a bottle of wine, and the past five years spun through my mind like a movie on fast-forward. "It's a constant eye-opener. I took so much for granted that was wrong." I poured two glasses, handed one to her.

"As if I didn't know! You were *such* an ass." She took a sip. "What made you change?"

"So who changed? I'm still George, just more enlightened. Okay, maybe with a hint of Georgia."

"I like Georgia better," she said.

"After what I've learned, I can't say I blame you. And now that I see things from, shall we say, a *different* perspective . . . it's more important than ever for me to be here on the Court.

"But I wanted to talk to you about something besides politics." I hesitated a moment. "You know I haven't had a relationship since my wife died. Well, all things change. I'm ready now."

"Good for you! Who's the lucky one?"

"It's . . . you." I took a deep breath and fought down the butterflies in my stomach and my words tumbled out, almost in a babble. "We could talk about it over lunch. That is, if you still want to. Have lunch with me, I mean." I felt my face get warm. I hadn't been this flustered since I asked

Mary Jane Allen to the high school prom sixty-three years ago.

"Why, Georgia, I didn't know!" Julie stood, raised her glass to me, and grinned. "I think it's a *grand* idea. Should be fun. But it does raise one question." She giggled. "Are you more George now, an old lech with a thing for young women, or Georgia? And, if you're Georgia, does that make you a les?"

Same old Julie . . . the tease! Who am I? Whether she knows it or not, she's zeroed in on the heart of the problem. At least, now I think I have an answer.

I shrugged. "All I know is, whether it's George or Georgia on the outside, in here . . . ," I put my hand on my chest, "it's just *me.*"

Duke Pennell traces his family tree along the ridges of the Ozarks, through the Cumberlands and the Smokies, back to the East Coast. He was raised on stories of the hills and their people, and now he tries to give back as good as he got.

Not What I Expected
By Steve Whisnant

Phil Graves crossed Spring River and turned right onto Highway 62B toward Main Street in downtown Hardy. Careful to avoid pedestrians, he eased down the road, then took a right and parked on Front Street. The crystal blue river flowed past town on the other side of a park and RV campsite.

The old, western-like hamlet had a reputation for antique shops along Main, and he planned to do some serious shopping. What compelled him to drive up from Batesville remained a mystery; it was not like him to take off so spontaneously. As an author of thirty books, and part-time professor at Lyon College, he had stories to write, research to do, and papers to grade. Now in his seventies, youthful motivation had seeped from his soul like wind erosion off a mountain. Perhaps he would find renewed energy today.

Inflated gas prices kept many travelers away, so he had little trouble avoiding sight seekers while strolling sidewalks along storefront shops. One business displayed unique animal gifts in the outside window. *Charlotte would have liked this store.* Dog costumes and other pet gag gifts hung from racks along the wall. He peered in. A poodle dressed as Dracula turned circles below its owner's feet.

Across the street he saw a sign that read Haunted Hotel. Stepping up steep wooden stairs, he entered and found a heavy-set gentleman behind a cash register, talking to tourists.

"...those ghost-buster guys did find several balls of energies throughout the hotel," he told the hooked listeners.

Graves passed them and walked up to a second floor where both hot dogs and popcorn were available for a dollar. Wooden floor panels creaked below his feet. From a hallway he peeked into a room where a guest had been killed by drunken gamblers back in the 1800s.

His wife would have enjoyed the history.

He descended stairs and walked back onto Main Street. In a large windowpane he noticed his reflection and tried to remember his youthful appearance. Thinning gray hair and loose, wrinkled skin along his forearms reminded him of a professor he knew last year forced to resign, due to age. Graves expected that same letter any day.

Something crawled along his exposed shin, and he reached down to swipe away an insect. His khaki shorts ended above his knees and he saw the old-man legs he remembered from when his grandfather was still alive. His now deceased sister and he would laugh and wonder why anyone would want to expose such ugly body parts.

At present, he was at least ten years older than Papaw had been. This thought used to make him laugh back in his sixties, but death loomed closer year after year. Now he was alone; his only daughter had married and moved to New Hampshire.

A few stores down from the Haunted Hotel he found a business he had never seen before in his previous trips. Opening the door, a bell jingled.

"Good morning," a clerk said. "May I help you?"

"Just browsing," he responded. He smiled and walked past, noticing her intense eyes follow him as he examined antiques on shelves throughout the room.

In a corner he saw stacks of old *Life* magazines, many dated from the late '30s when he was born. Wood-plank shelves lined a wall, adorned with glass bowls and figurines of all shapes and sizes. A few items looked like objects Charlotte had kept behind a glass door in an old cabinet in their front room.

A pair of salt and pepper shakers in shapes of white cows with black polka-dots sat beside artistic plates with Rockwell prints. Graves picked up the pepper container and strong images of a boy swinging on a tire over a river flooded his mind. With shaking hands, he quickly set the cow back on the shelf.

He glanced around the establishment, afraid he might have had a stroke. When he realized it was his imagination, he reached for the saltshaker.

Visions of a mom putting breakfast on a table popped into his mind. Graves held the porcelain object in both hands and could hear the gentle conversation between son and mom. They talked of school, farm work, and fishing on Saturday morning.

He put the shaker back and moved forward. His rapidly beating heart and sweaty palms forced him to pay close attention to his health. He moved away from glass cabinets. If he were about to go into cardiac arrest, he wanted to have some control where he fell, not make a scene by breaking delicate antiques.

After awhile, he recovered and felt it safe to continue. A red bowl drew him. He wiped his hands on his shorts, then picked up the glass object with care and examined the hand-painted design. A video began to play inside his mind. He saw a farm scene atop a mountain in the Ozarks. A woman in long dress clipped damp laundry to a clothesline strung from a rustic home to a cedar.

Two sisters played with Raggedy Ann dolls beside a barn where a mule stuck its head over a wooden fence. He returned the bowl and the vision vanished.

He had once written a novel about a man with special powers, and now wondered if he was dreaming he had turned into his character. Would he soon wake up? Did he too have control of his fantasies, and if so, could he send his conscious anywhere in the universe? Could he talk to Charlotte?

These ideas circled within his mind as he reached for a straw doll. An evil image of a man, with dark, marble-like eyes, formed. Graves saw the man lean down, his hand rubbed his daughter's inner thigh. "This is between you and me, okay? Don't tell Mommy."

Graves threw the shredded toy back upon the shelf. A green plastic toy soldier, on his knees with his rifle pointed forward, caught his attention. He picked it up and saw the same man punch his son in the jaw beside a river shoal. "You must know the fear of God!" he said.

Graves set down the play warrior. *They were brother and sister.*

The shop clerk walked past, carrying a tray of silverware.

"Excuse me," Graves said. "Where do you get these items?"

"Some folks bring them in, but most are purchased from estate sales."

"Because of bankruptcy?"

"Sometimes, but usually it's death."

"Oh."

A cast iron frying pan sat atop stacks of Zane Grey novels. He reached for the thick handle and experienced a woman cooking at a wood-heated stove. The fuzzy feeling faded and he sensed a different woman, now preparing dinner at an electric range. Perhaps the daughter took possession of the iron pan after her mother's death?

The stack of the famous author's books reached waist high. *I can't believe Zane wrote this many novels.*

Flipping through a copy, he felt the eyes of numerous readers over the years. Many sat in swings under oaks, along an Ozark ridge, enjoying the Western tale. The books had probably been passed down over generations until the final owner lost them to consignment. Pages were faded to an off-white, and many covers were worn or ripped and repaired with tape, but he felt there were still many years of reading left for the volumes, now stacked on a dirty floor.

Glass and bronze candleholders stood on a shelf above the novels. *TV Guides* from the '70s sat upright behind them. Careful to pick up an empty holder, he saw etched into the bottom base: To Kinney and Phillip. Hope you have many wonderful years in your marriage. May 24, 1925.

As he read the phrase, images of the couple's life formed in his mind. He sensed their love, parenthood, children, and death. How long he stood there reliving their past he did not know. A sound behind him brought him to the present.

"Sir, are you okay?"

Graves replaced the candleholder. "Yes ... just daydreaming, I guess. What time do you close?"

"We never close, we're open 24/7."

"A consignment shop?"

"We have a lot of customers."

Many pieces lay in the aisle and he had to step over them; clothes that had fallen off a rack; necklaces dangled from hooks. Antique watches and pocketknives, with price tags connected by a thin string, lined shelves.

In a bookcase, partly covered by stained pillows, he found an assortment of paperbacks. The first novel he reached for sent impressions of a woman, never married, who had spent her life in a mobile home along a hillside. Many afternoons she sat in a rusted metal chair reading her books.

A familiar title with red and yellow spine caught his attention. His painful arthritic fingers struggled to free this nonfiction hardback lodged between volumes shelved snuggly on the case. As he opened it and brought the small print to his eyes, his life flashed before him like caricatures on a flip-pad. Mom and Dad. He felt like he could reach out and touch them. Then he saw a boyhood dog he had loved, and finally his graduation from high school in Mountain View, and college at Fayetteville.

Old lovers raced through his mind until Charlotte settled in. Images of their first date in an Italian restaurant near Tontitown, and finally marriage and a daughter born in Batesville. Scenes hurried through his mind like he was watching a movie on an old projector, when the click, click,

click stopped him cold. A sound of the reel tape slapping itself repeated as he remembered that day Charlotte was admitted into hospice. Then the tombstone and his loneliness; the last impression he received was falling asleep last night. Then the clairvoyant-link faded.

He glanced inside the hardback cover and saw his name inscribed in the upper corner. He had recently given away boxes of books. He set the volume down with trembling hands and returned to the front. *Where's the owner?*

Outside the glass windows he could see tourists shopping along Main Street. He exited the business and rushed back on unsteady legs to his car. Perspiration dotted his face and armpits. *Time to go home.*

At Cave City, he took Highway 230 toward Strawberry, his wife's childhood birthplace. The haunting images he experienced in the antique shop compelled him to visit her grave. Highway 230 turned into Route 25 to Saffell.

A funeral procession blocked his way soon after he drove through Strawberry. He stopped to watch the vehicles turn onto the dirt road leading up a treeless mountain. When the last car passed, he pulled in behind it. In a pasture enclosed by a barbed wire fence, he saw a couple embrace by a pond, its banks covered with cows.

A canvas marquee tent stood erect over a grave, far away from where Charlotte rested. The line of mourners gathered there as Graves stopped his car a distance from them and approached his wife's tombstone.

The granite monument displayed her name and date of birth and death. Beside it, etched into the stone, was his name and birth date. All that remained to be carved into the headstone was his date of death.

A single oak stood a hundred yards away. When he glanced toward it, he saw Charlotte as he remembered her on their first date. Her flowery dress flapped against the mountain breeze, brunette hair brushed her shoulders.

Past rows of tombstones, he walked toward her opened arms.

Steve Whisnant is a happily married father of three daughters, and has equally been blessed with over 95 writing contest wins. Two of his four books are anthologies of his award-winning short stories. For details of his writing career go to his website: www.stevewhisnant.com.

Tim, the Radar Man
By Ralph H. Herron

On March 1st, 1953, Corporal Timothy J. Mahoney arrived at the 606th Aircraft Control and Warning Squadron. Korea was his first assignment as a radar technician outside of the States. Tim had grown up on a farm in North Dakota and joined the Air Force looking for adventure. Even though he was approaching his twenty first birthday, between his slim build and very blonde hair, he looked like he might be fifteen or sixteen. We soon learned that looks can be very deceiving.

The 606th was located on the top of a mountain called Old Smokey. Smokey was located just a few miles from the Kimpo Airport, also known as K-14 by the military. Kimpo was the home of a squadron of American Sabre Jet Fighters. They were responsible for protecting all of the air space in the northern half of South Korea. Tracking enemy aircraft was a routine activity for us, unless that aircraft was headed south. Then the 606th was placed on immediate alert.

The most essential component of the 606th was radar. By using it effectively the technicians were able to identify and follow any aircraft flying in their area of responsibility. One radar tech laughed and told me that their equipment was so precise they could tell what an enemy pilot had for breakfast.

We soon learned that Tim was a fun person to be around and he fit right in. He had a great sense of humor and loved to tell us humorous incidents that happened to him. But more important, he was one of the most articulate and precise technicians. It seemed like nothing got to him and every incident was, to him, a real challenge. When he sat in front of that radar screen it was like he zoned out of everything around him and nothing could break his concentration. Regardless of the pressure, he remained solid. And we were about to find out why.

In addition to what seemed to be more enemy activity than usual that month, there were a couple of incidents that created a lot of excitement on Old Smokey. It seemed to be a strange coincidence that during both episodes Tim was the tech on duty.

Twice during March radar picked up unidentified flying objects (UFO), tracked them, and alerted K-14 to send up Sabres to intercept and attempt to identify them. Both times it happened at night. Because the 606th recorded and later transcribed all radio transmissions between the pilots and their home base, we had an accurate record of what happened. The Sabre Jets would get close enough to pick up the UFOs on radar and visually see their lights. And then, as the Sabres got closer to those objects that appeared to be just hanging in space with no movement, the UFO would suddenly go straight up and out of radar at a speed that could not be calculated. According to the radar techs, the objects were faster than anything man made. There was a lot of speculation about what they were and who they were...friend or foe? Our base commander even received calls from the Pentagon.

When Tim was questioned about the incidents, his reaction to questions was very simple and direct. "We have been honored to see a glimpse of the future," he replied. It was becoming more obvious that Tim, the guy who loved to laugh and tell humorous stories, had a side that was much deeper than any of us realized. He daily demonstrated a personal belief in his own abilities and a faith that was so strong that it appeared to be the motivating force in his life.

The weather the last week in March was no different than the first week. There was a lot of rain, thunder storms, and fog. Tim was working nights that last week of the month and one night it seemed like everything that could go wrong did. Two Sabres had been sent from K-14 over to the east coast of Korea to check on some unusual ground activity in a disputed area. Before they reached their target one of the Sabres developed a malfunction and had to return to base. That left the pilot of the remaining Sabre, a Captain Martin, to proceed alone. He completed his mission and was returning to K-14 when Tim's radar picked up two enemy MiG Fighters closing in on the Captain. One MiG was on his left and the other MiG was on his right.

Martin tried to shake them off with defensive maneuvers but none of them worked. The MiGs kept moving in for the kill. K-14 could send up support but by the time they got there it would be too late. Back at the 606th Tim's supervisor, Sergeant Moore, was monitoring the situation. He told Tim that Captain Martin was "dead meat, he doesn't have a chance." Tim disagreed and told the Sergeant that he knew that the Captain would land safely. Sergeant Moore just shook his head, turned, and walked out of the room, leaving Tim alone at his radar work station.

The transcription of what happened next was probably read by more guys at the 606th than the latest issue of *Stars and Stripes Magazine*.

Tim: Captain Martin, I am aware of the situation that you are in. I can bring you through this, Sir, but you must do exactly what I tell you to do. Do you understand?

Martin: Roger.

Tim: Maintain your speed but descend one thousand feet now.

Martin: Done

Tim: The next direction I give you will be to turn thirty degrees to the right and immediately go straight up. Do you understand?

Martin: Roger. (Pause)

Tim: Do it now! (Pause) Both MiGs are now off the radar. Do you have a visual?

Captain: Roger. I see two fireballs on the mountain.

Tim: Those fireballs are the two MiGs. Return to base, Sir.

Three days later Captain Martin got a jeep and driver to transport him up to the 606th on Smokey. He thanked Tim for saving his life and showed him pictures of his wife and two children. Then Tim said, "Sir, I really can't take full responsibility for your safety.

"But you were the only person I talked to," he replied.

"That's correct, Sir," said Tim. "But I was only following the instructions that I was given."

The Captain appeared to be confused. "So who gave you those instructions?"

"Let me explain, Sir," answered Tim. "Any time I sit down in front of that radar screen I am very aware that what I do or don't do, what I say or don't say, will have a very positive or negative effect on peoples' lives. The first time I talked to you I knew that the directions that I was about to give you were correct. I knew that if you would do what I told you to do that you would be alright.

"Well," said the Captain, "I'm glad that you did because when you told me to descend 1000 feet I wasn't so sure. That put me down between mountains instead of staying above them."

"Yes Sir, that is correct. I knew that there were mountains in the area where you were flying and I knew that at your speed and in the dark you would not be able to see them in time to avoid them. But neither would the MiG pilots. When I told you to take the thirty degree turn and go straight up I knew that at that moment it was the safe thing for you to do."

"Okay," replied the Captain. "You were right. I am standing here now because you were right. But how did you know?"

"Sir," Tim replied, "as a pilot and an officer you have learned the importance of taking directions and following orders. I have also learned how importance obedience is. For whatever reason, Sir, He (Tim pointed up) protected you. I just did what He told me to do."

The Captain Martin episode became part of the 606th history and legend. For the rest of the time that Tim was on Old Smokey, any time that he was asked about it, his response was that he felt honored to have been part of the Captain's flying experience testimony.

Dr. Herron is an educator who has worked as a secondary language arts teacher, counselor, building principal, and special education director. In addition to writing a weekly newspaper article and various stories, he is a published playwright. He has directed and produced numerous plays and musicals. Dr. Herron and his wife, Janice, reside at Lake Ozark.

The Coon Hunting Contest
By Nancy Hartney

Leroy Jackson moved his ponderous frame toward the table under the ancient oaks. He had a pronounced limp in his right leg, wore greasy bib overalls and led a deep copper-colored hound on a frayed rope.

"Y'all men give me one of them there sign-up forms." He drawled in a demanding tone and his left cheek bulged with chewing tobacco, creating brown drool which crept into the creases around his mouth. He didn't wipe.

One of the men behind the table glanced up. "Hello, Leroy. That Queenie you got with you? Need one form, do you?"

Leroy grunted. He took the registration paper with grime caked fingers and laboriously filled in the blanks, stopping often to lick his pencil stub. He did not bother to step away from the table, requiring the men behind to shuffle around his bulk for their forms.

The hound sat at his feet, yawned, then stretched out, head on her paws. Her copper coat, common to Redbones, mirrored the autumn light. She sported two white toes on one foot and a small white patch on her chest.

The sun dripped through the tree branches, pooling in tiny drops of umber and orange among the leaves. Cars and trucks, parked askew in the oak grove, marked spots where folks set up their camps. A giant bonfire, laid in the middle of the field, would be lit at dark as a summons to the bluegrass fiddlers, hunters and others.

Leroy, locally known as a bootlegger, carried a stench of meanness about him. He had been married three times to straight-laced, good Christian women, each who left in turn, either by dying or running off. He never seemed to notice or be bothered by their leaving. One thing for certain though, he loved hunting and was unashamedly proud of his hound.

Now, at seventy-four, he aimed to win the Ozark Hills and Hollows Coon Dog Hunt Contest. It was to be his last great endeavor.

Leroy handed his form to the same fellow behind the table.

"Well, you know the rules," the man said accepting the paper. "You draw cards for your night, go out with whoever draws with you, and the judge follows. Y'all bring in all the coon tags you can get before sun-up. Judge will score on which hound strikes, barks up first, stays treed and your coons."

Again, Leroy grunted. His great bushy eyebrows hid his eyes. He mostly lived outdoors, so had the craggy look that harsh weather pounds into a face.

Moving off toward the edge of the campground, he sat down next to a pine tree, flopped his gunny sack nearby and carefully laid his rifle across it. He ate cold biscuits and fried fatback, sharing with his dog. He drank deeply from his crock knowing it'd be only a few short hours before the evening drawing.

Leroy stretched out on a ragged quilt. Queenie curled beside him. He laid a calloused hand on her head and softly scratched around her ears. It was the only gentleness he allowed himself to show, and then only if no one was near.

He slept through the bonfire lighting, pre-hunt bragging and banjo picking. He woke with a start, struggled to his feet, and hobbled stiffly toward the ash-sparks floating into the night sky, grimacing with the effort. The crowd had gathered around the hunt officials in the orange firelight.

"Now, men," said a monitor, "we draw numbers. Whatever your number, that's the night you go out. Single entries get paired up by the drawing. Four teams go out separately each night with a judge in different directions, on different sides of the river. Everybody needs to take their own light and gun."

Numbers got drawn and the men shuffled around. Leroy drew a three; he'd go out Wednesday night with Paul Irving from near Pineville.

At fourteen, Paul relished hunting. His ma had named him after the biblical Paul, saying that no matter where he traveled he'd help folks along the way. His grandpa taught him hunting.

Weighing less than forty pounds, Paul's clay colored hound, Daisy Mae, appeared almost dainty. Because she was the smallest in a litter of eleven, she was not sold. Instead, she had been given to Paul, to make what he could out of her, rather than knocked in the head as culls sometimes were.

"Gawd damn whelp of a kid. I ain't come this way to hunt with no runt dog and a still-wet youn'un," Leroy bellowed. He stalked toward the officials, pushed his huge belly forward, his voice demanding and hard.

"Re-draw. I ain't huntin' with them two. Queenie's a coon huntin' hound not no dern training hound. This here ain't right."

The officials stared at Leroy. Finally one said "You know the rules. It really doesn't matter who a hound goes out with, the judge's decision goes to the first hound to strike, move out on a track, bark up, stay treed until called off and how many coons. You can go with who you drew or you can quit the contest. Up to you."

Leroy glared at the man and flung a murderous look at those gathered. "Y'all ought not to let kids in this thing. They ain't earned no rights." He stomped off, black with rage.

On Wednesday, the wind picked up and took on a frigid edge. Metal-gray storm clouds roiled over the gathering as dark descended.

When Leroy and Queenie with Paul and Daisy stepped up to the starting point, the crowd hushed, waiting to see if he would create another fuss. He didn't, but he deliberately stepped on Paul's foot as he shoved past.

Reeve Davis, a Missouri man, was assigned as their judge. "Leroy you've done this before and you know the rules. Paul, this is your first big competition. Just keep in mind the things your grandpa taught you. Trust the hound and let her do the hunting. I'll keep the score."

Reeve looked off into the dark. "Cold ground holds scent pretty good but this wind scatters it. That means the hounds have to work harder. Let's get moving."

The three men with the two hounds walked toward the river. Spectators followed to the bank and clustered together but went no further.

Leroy unleashed Queenie ahead of Paul and walked off along the bank toward the west, not looking back. Daisy ran to Queenie as soon as she was set loose, and jumped about, face-licking and whining. Queenie tolerated the attention for a few minutes before settling down, nose to ground, her tail flagging as she worked.

Several hundred yards down the river, she opened, bawling her excitement and charging through the underbrush. Daisy honored, running close behind. The judge, Leroy and Paul stood listening then followed the hound song to the edge of a cornfield, not far from the river.

Leroy fell behind in the trappy undergrowth, struggled to keep up, and paused frequently to catch his breath. He felt his gimp leg throbbing and silently cursed the pain.

Reeve Davis and Paul hurried ahead, keeping as close to the hounds as possible. Queenie's bawl deepened and grew aggressive. Daisy's chop played under-chords.

At a lone hickory tree, a third of the way into the cornfield, Reeve and Paul found the hounds barking up, moaning, teeth clicking. They stood and watched, then moved forward, shining lights into the tree.

"We need to wait on Leroy." Reeve looked back across the field. "I think the corn stubble is holding him up."

Finally, Leroy stumbled in, breathing hard and unable to talk.

"Paul, you take the shot. Queenie was strike hound. Both hounds stayed treed." Reeve wrote his decision in the judge notebook.

After the shot, Paul held Daisy's collar, calming her down with, "Dead coon. Dead coon. Good hound. Good hound. Dead coon."

Queenie hesitated, backed off the still animal, whined and looked at Leroy. He limped over to the dead coon, nudged it with his boot, releasing her with "Good girl. Dead coon."

The men leashed the hounds and walked a steep hillside with a deep narrow holler and bluff bench parallel to the river. As soon as they were set loose, both dogs, running shoulder to shoulder, scoured north through the brush before dropping off the dirt bank into the thickets. It was not long before their music signaled another track running down and over the ridgeline.

This time, having to climb up before sliding down, Leroy moved even slower. His great weight, poor balance and gimp leg made him grimace in pain.

The judge and Paul arrived first. Two half-grown coons were treed. They waited on Leroy.

"Queenie got strike points; Daisy treed. Both hounds stayed." Reeve held his light high to catch the reflection in the raccoons' eyes. "You want the shot or should Paul take it again?"

"I'm gonna take it." Despite the cold Leroy was sweating and breathing hard. He cocked his rifle, fired, missed the first shot, but got the highest coon with a clean second one. He botched the third try. The coon dropped drunkenly from the tree and attempted to crawl away. Queenie lunged forward and, with a clean neck snap, dispatched the wounded animal.

"I ain't in the habit missing a shot. Huntin' with some fool little dog done throw'd me off." Leroy bent down to stoke Queenie's head as if apologizing to her.

Paul stood quietly with Daisy then slipped the rope on her.

"Mr. Leroy, I'm sorry you don't like me and Daisy but she's a good hound. My grandpa taught me hunting. He told me 'trust the hound.' I'm gonna do that."

Reeve smiled and nodded agreement. "Looks to me like they make a fine pair working off each other. They got three coons and both have points."

Leroy snorted. "My hound got no need for some half-growed cull hunting." He spun on his heel and walked toward the river. The judge shrugged and followed. The boy and his hound trailed behind.

The wind picked up and a light drizzle began. Still, it was only two o'clock, six hours before sun-up, with plenty of time for another cast. The trio walked to the greasy bottoms along the river where willow and birch crowded the bank, dragging finger-like limbs in the water. Small sand bars here and there offered prime coon forage sites.

As soon as the hounds were unleashed, they opened. Scent, hot enough to make them scream, drew both animals under the weeping trees, back and forth, back and forth, scouring along the river edge. Queenie figured it out first. She let loose one long howl and jumped into the water, swimming toward a gravel bar.

The men, following along the bank, stumbled over vines and dead limbs. Leroy tripped and dropped his light. "Damn dark. Can't hardly see nothing." Mud sucked at his boots, slowing him even more.

Hound music grew sweet then descended into a snarling fracas. Queenie found a bull coon feeding on the sandbar and grabbed it by the haunch. He whipped around and grabbed her in a death grip. They were entwined in a slobbering ball of blood and hair.

Daisy, following the older hound, pulled herself up on the bar just as the old bull broke loose. He dove for the channel. Queenie shook her head splattering blood on the rocks and leaped into the water only steps behind the ringtail.

The coon had not gotten to his size and age without learning a trick or two. He lured Queenie into the fast current, turned back into her face and climbed cat-like on her head. His weight forced her down while he rode above the water. She fought to keep from drowning.

A savage will to live pulsed through both animals. Every time the hound's head frantically broke the surface, the coon shifted his weight, biting, scratching, forcing her under again and again.

Waist-high in the river, the men squinted through the dark watching a shadowy outline of the grim contest.

Leroy screamed his rage. "I can't shoot the sumbitch. I'm libel to hit Queenie." He stumbled against rocks hidden under the water and fell hard. He sank, sputtering and gagging as weight and wet overalls dragged him downstream.

Reeve dropped his light, ducked under, grabbed Leroy by his straps, and pulled him back toward the bank. Paul waded toward the men, looped his hand around a strap and pulled with all his young strength.

Leroy flailed and screamed, "Get my hound. Gawd-damn it all to hell, get my hound. Leave me be."

Just as the men reached the dark bank, they tripped on a pile of deadwood, going under, entangled in the limbs. Paul and Reeve held on to Leroy's straps and pulled him up as they thrashed about to find solid footing.

"Get my hound. Get my hound." Leroy coughed. He felt his legs give way again. Unable to help himself, he kept flailing, "Get my Queenie. Leave me be. Gawd, get my hound. Don't let that coon drown her."

Daisy, exhausted from her struggle, plunged back into the river, swimming toward the hunted and the hunter in their watery struggle. With a lurch, she grabbed the old bull by his haunch. Snarling, he jumped off the older hound's head and paddled toward a dead tree lying across the water, hauling the young hound with him.

Dragging himself out of the water, he twisted back into Daisy's face. Confused, she immediately loosened her grip and was swept downstream.

Queenie, weak but free of the weight of the coon, swam with the current.

Drizzle turned to rain, heavy and pounding. Hell's own blackness shrouded the primal contest.

Reeve had pulled Leroy's head above water. He part shoved, part hauled the older man up the embankment, yelling at Paul. "Get the hounds. You got to get them before the rain brings the river up. I can manage this feller."

Paul waded back into the current screaming. "Daisy! Get to. Get to. Here. Here." A frantic edge crept into his voice. "Come hound. Come Daisy."

The two hounds whined and paced from one side of the far bend to the other, seeming to make a decision whether to continue after the coon or swim to the boy. Finally, Daisy, then Queenie, jumped into the water and paddled toward Paul. He waded out as far as possible, waited for them, grabbed each collar and slopped toward high ground.

It was broad daylight before Reeve could summon help from the hunt officials and get Leroy trucked out.

Paul brought the hounds in, petting their blood-stained faces. "Y'all good girls. Good hunters. We'll get another coon some other time." Once back at camp, he kept an arm slung around both she-dogs, one on either side of him.

Reeve went out the next several nights helping to judge the last of the contestants. Two brothers from Oklahoma won the contest on Friday.

Leroy had several busted ribs, a broken hand and a wrenched knee. Worse, he caught pneumonia. Since he'd run off his latest woman and even his grown children, he found himself hard pressed to care for Queenie. She ended up tied in his barn. Although he hobbled out each evening to feed and pet her, he was shame ridden about her care.

Paul took Daisy home to his mother who was an old hand at sewing up dogs. Within the week, the pair was out hunting squirrels during daylight and coons at night.

One afternoon, a good year later, Paul looked up to see Leroy's pick-up rattling toward the house. A hound box bounced around in the bed. Daisy rushed out from under the porch steps to bark, announcing the arrival. Paul stepped off the front stoop. His ma stood in the door way.

Leroy parked under the oak at the edge of the yard. He stuck his arm out the truck window and fumbled for the outside door handle. It took long minutes for him to haul his great frame out of the truck, gimp along the running board, and prop himself against the fender.

"I come here 'bout my hound." He struggled getting the tailgate down and fumbled opening the hound box. Queenie sashayed out, tail wagging, licking at him.

Daisy sat on her haunches and cut loose with a bay ever so often. The boy walked into the yard, eyes wide. His ma stepped out on the sagging porch.

Leroy stared off into the woods and fields surrounding the weather-beaten house, listening to bird calls and squirrel chatter. He remained silent a long time.

"I can't get 'round no more. These ribs ain't healed right and my crippled leg acts up bad. Still got this here cough. I can't walk them woods like I done. I'm reckon my day has passed."

He paused and spit out a wad of tobacco. "It ain't no life for a huntin' dog to lay up in a pen or be tied up all the time. They gotta be out. They gotta hunt. It's they nature."

He paused and took a deep breath. "I'm gonna give Queenie to you. You hunt her. You an' that there little runt hound. They a good pair." He stroked Queenie's head, petting around her ears and down her neck.

"I never could rightly tolerate them women I married. Don't think I cared much for them youn'uns neither. But I do care for this here hound." His hand lingered on her head.

Then, with that, he pivoted painfully back into the truck cab, slammed the door and rattled off down the road, leaving a rooster-tail of dust.

Queenie gave out with one long, mournful note. It carried across the fields and into the trees. She sat looking down the road, then turned and trotted off with the little hound.

Nancy Hatney's bio can be found on pg. 94.

More Than Fruitcake
By Nancy Hartney

*U*sually about first cold snap, Granny and Granddaddy, on their way from Atlanta to West Palm Beach for the winter, arrived at the farm.

Just in time to make fruitcakes. Those days, fruitcake was a staple and expected Christmas gift. It was Tradition.

We'd all gather around the rough kitchen table, drinking coffee, or, in the case of me and the younger cousins, cups of half milk and half coffee with spoons of sugar. I'd help empty packages of candied fruits, dark raisins, nuts, cinnamon, spices, and dates from the grocery sacks. Floured cloths got laid out, bowls lined up and scissors and knives readied. Momma, Aunt Grace Rose and Granny did the measuring and mixing. The older cousins started the chopping. Me and the younger cousins took on washing the bowls, knives and making sure the dishwater was kept hot.

My Aunt Grace Rose, who pulled her hair straight back into a hard little bun at the nape of her neck, usually started it – 'it' being the latest community gossip. When she talked, her freckled face glowed red and her hands flew about. In fact, she spoke with more animation than the rest of the Davis women put together.

"Well, Bethany and Lester were at it again. Sheriff Moore had to go out there Saturday night. By the time Sheriff got out there, Bethany's eye was already swole shut. 'Course Lester denied touching her. But talk has it he smelled of whiskey real bad."

"I heard Sheriff finally drove back to town and left them there." The tight lines around Granny's old eyes betrayed her anger. "Now I know Sheriff thinks stuff like that's a private family matter, but he did say he'd haul Lester in if'n Bethany pressed charges on him. Why that girl doesn't leave that man, I don't know." Granny, who could only be described as ponderous, would go on. "It scares those kids to death when Lester gets mean. That oldest one, John Lee, jes' might jump him one day. He's as tall as Lester now and he don't like the way that man treats his mother."

My momma, the beauty of the family with her chestnut hair, had a sweet way about her that disarmed the most acid tongue. "Y'all remember now, Lester provides good for the family when he's working. His handsome good looks and sweet-talking ways have been good for Bethany. Especially since she's always thought of herself as plain. Trouble only starts when he gets into the bottle."

"He uses those ways to keep his job too. If something happened to Lester it would leave Bethany and those six kids struggling." Aunt Grace Rose wiped spilled flour off the table. "Lordy, who knows? They might be better off."

"God love her but she's got her hands full with twin babies." Momma had a slow, rich accent. "She's really smart and could do most anything, given the chance."

"Goodness mercy, yes." Granny groped for a dish towel. "Lester's got a silver tongue and a dark mean streak. Bethany ought to up and leave him."

Talk went on as we cracked nuts. Since we had pecan trees, we used pecans mostly although a few almonds, Brazil nuts and walnuts got store bought. The nuts added a special crunch, balancing out the semi-soft sweetness of the candied fruits.

"By the way, did you hear Mary Ann Henderson, Jolene Sloan's mother, was over in the county hospital last week? Seems she has some kind of stomach problem. Again." Aunt Grace Rose could never just work. She liked to talk no matter what she did.

Mary Ann and Jolene were members of the Piney Grove Baptist Church, not our congregation, but Momma saw them buying groceries at the Winn-Dixie and during school PTA meetings. I knew Sylvia Sloan, Jolene's daughter, from school. She was eleven, like me.

"What's John Guy doing? Maybe we ought to take by meals for him." Momma could never stand something in need.

To her credit, Aunt Grace Rose could keep her hands busy and talk at the same time. "Jolene has been taking her daddy over his meals. But you know him. He won't even heat water. That man's worthless when it comes to kitchen stuff."

Granny raised her eyebrows. "This is *not* the first time Mary has been in with stomach trouble. He worries her to death. Pastor Gerald needs to visit and get the church involved. That'll please Mary and set John Guy to fuming."

Talk droned on, and the chopping and flouring continued. I listened intently to these women.

Momma measured out homemade butter, brown sugar, and flour. She cracked eggs and separated the deep-yellow yolks. She had strong hands and could cream the batter real smooth.

Aunt Grace Rose began greasing the tube pans. "Well, talk has it that Lydia Smith got caught at the Red Rooster Diner picking up a trucker from out toward Suwannee County. That caused a set to. Her husband's fit to be tied and talking about moving the whole family off to the panhandle."

Momma glanced up. "Well, Lydia sings in the Methodist Church choir and she's got a beautiful voice. Dwayne's good to help at the rest home, make repairs for people and church usher on Sundays. All said and done, they are good people."

Granny ignored the statement. "That woman runs around with anything in pants. Can't figure out how her and him got together in the first place. Lord knows he's boring as a fence post."

When everything had been cut, chopped, and measured, Momma folded the nuts and fruit into the batter and filled the pans. Then, being the more artistic, she dipped whole pieces of candied pineapple rings, cherry halves, and almonds in Karo syrup and arranged them flower-like on top.

With everything in the oven, Granny Jones poured herself another cup of coffee. She took it black, no sugar. "Did you hear tell Felton Davis went and got a job at the pulpwood mill over to Valdosta?"

Aunt Grace Rose poured herself coffee, stirred in cream and watched the color change. "It will be a long drive for Felton everyday and he probably won't last, but I know Bea will be glad for the money however long it lasts. Felton don't like to do anything for long except fool with his hounds. Good thing Bea has her job down at Winn-Dixie."

I thought hard about that. Bea was one of the few women who worked outside the home. Her country looks hid a tenacious, unconventional heart. Little did I realize she was a modern woman in a homemade flour-sack dress.

With most of the washing up done and the cakes baking, us cousins scooted out to poke around the corn crib for snakes and dig through the hay stacks.

I'd pondered on the kitchen talk. Being young come with problems but, then again, being grown-up did too. Seemed to me it didn't get better, only more complicated.

By late afternoon, the pans got pulled from the oven and clean flour sacks spread out. Granny lightly drizzled whiskey over the cakes before gently wrapping them in liquor soaked cloths and storing them in huge lard tins. Odors, so strong I tasted them, lingered in the warm kitchen until late evening. It would be the Christmas holidays before the cans could be opened and the seasoned, moist cakes pulled out.

Throughout the years, Granny, Momma, and Aunt Grace Rose gathered to make the fruitcakes. I graduated high school, moved to a bigger city, shaking off the farm dust. My cousins married. Some stayed around north Florida. Some moved up to Atlanta and others down to Lake City. Sometimes they came back with their new husbands and babies, visiting and showing off, claiming they'd come to help with the fruitcakes.

Those times, talk ranged over the family and neighbors, who lost their job, got divorced, got married, or had yet another baby. Who was sick and needed help, who missed church Sunday last, when was the next homecoming-dinner-on-the-ground, and who died and how the funeral went. Even when I had heard stuff earlier, it was nonetheless told again.

Looking back, I never realized how quickly time changed, dragging the years behind. New families moved in. My local high school integrated in the '70s. Farms were sold to big producers. Pastor Gerald got called to a church near Panama City. The Red Rooster Diner burned down one night during a summer storm. Arson was suspected but no one ever proved it.

Mamma called me with the news that John Guy was plowing when his tractor slipped near a gully and rolled. Mary moved in with her daughter Jolene after the old man died. I heard she never did have any more stomach trouble. Sheriff Moore retired and his deputy, Garth Miller, got elected.

It puzzled me that Bethany and Lester were still together. Bethany got her brood up and off on their own. The twins moved to Alabama, got married to real nice girls. The two middle ones went as far as North Carolina to find jobs and start families. The oldest girl graduated from community college and moved to Jacksonville. She never married. John Lee never married neither. He moved to Live Oak, a neighboring town, to be around if his mother needed him.

Momma told me that, with everyone gone, Bethany went into nurse training. She waited tables to earn her night school money. When she finished up, the county hospital hired her.

Lester kept drinking. His good looks began to fade. He'd show up late for work or else didn't show up at all. He got fired from near ever place in our three-county area. The drinking got worse, especially as months became years.

One morning he got up, made coffee and waited for Bethany to come home from the night shift. He shot her dead as soon as she walked in the door, and then called Sheriff Miller. Bethany still had on her nurse uniform. She had finally left Lester.

Aunt Grace Rose told me about it during a visit home. This time, while she talked, her hands were still. She just gripped her coffee cup real hard.

Granny Jones sighed deep, her huge breasts rising with the effort. "Lester couldn't stand Bethany having a job, making her own money and not needing him no more. His meanness just took over."

"I guess there are different kinds of needs and love." Momma's voice got softer. "Those two were bound by rough times. Hard to say if they stayed married out of love or need or helplessness. For certain, they all took the bitter and sweet together."

Granny moved in with a daughter in Atlanta when Granddaddy passed. Aunt Grace Rose left for central Florida where it was warmer. Bea moved into town and got promoted to fresh produce manager. Felton stayed in the woods with his hounds. Momma died. Daddy sold the farm and went to live down the panhandle near Steinhatchee. He hung on a year or two, then slipped away unnoticed. I lived in Memphis, Ashville, Dallas, and, for a brief time, Chicago.

After Momma passed, I didn't go back home. I gradually lost touch with the cousins and the community, although those piney woods and hardscrabble farms still hang in my memory. I often hear a chill wind rattle through dry corn fields, a door banging against its rotted frame, or stately oaks groaning under their burden of years.

I don't make fruitcake any more. Nonetheless, the taste makes me think of home and that gathering of women.

Today, most folks don't remember fruitcake, or they think of it as a too heavy holiday thing stacked on display at Wal-Mart. Some city types buy it as a gourmet item baked by monks at a Missouri monastery. Other folks like to mail order it from the Collins Street Bakery over in Texas.

But I remember real, homemade fruitcake. I can smell it baking. I can taste the sweetness against bitter black coffee. I think of it as winter grows deep and Christmas arrives. The chunky fruit and the crunchy nuts, like my hometown, are bound together by a dark-spice batter of joy and rough times, smelling slightly of whiskey.

Nancy Hartney regularly contributes articles and photographs to *The Chronicle of the Horse*, *Sidelines*, and the *Horsemen's Roundup*. Her book reviews have appeared in the *Ft.Worth Star Telegram*, motorcycle touring pieces and photographs in *American Iron* and general articles in the *Northwest Arkansas Times*. While continuing to write non-fiction, she has turned her pen to fiction. She lives in Fayetteville, Arkansas.

Changes
By Alan Zacher

The situation came to a climax last Wednesday, October 14th, at precisely 6 p.m. in the spacious living room of our penthouse apartment , at the exact moment the theme music for *The McNeil/Lehrer Hour* wafted across the room from the high-quality speakers of our almost half-a-wall size color television. Located two inches from the north inner wall, it is six feet from the low, wooden-framed antique coffee table, which is three feet from our long, black leather sofa. All the furniture was precisely arranged to take full advantage of the sun shining through the diaphanous white drapes on the two ornate French doors on the east wall that overlook downtown St. Louis.

I was totally unaware, until that precise moment, that we had a "situation." It had been a usual Wednesday, with Sarah and I rising at our designated hour—5 a.m. on the dot. We showered, dressed, and were eating our breakfast at the kitchen dinette table while reading The Wall Street Journal—well,, while I read The Wall Street Journal. The breakfast consisted of our daily one-minute boiled egg, a slice of toasted wheat bread, a small bowl of Special K cornflakes, a glass of freshly squeezed orange juice, followed by a single cup of freshly ground coffee—Columbian bean.

We went to work—she to the marketing/advertising agency and me to the accounting firm—did a full day of work, then returned home at precisely 5 p.m. We ate our designated Wednesday evening meal—baked filet of cod with a dab of tartar sauce, lima beans, a freshly tossed salad with red vinaigrette dressing, accompanied by a light white wine.

We removed our China plates, crystal glasses, cloth napkins, and silverware from the dining room and cleaned everything up, then retired to the living room. She sat at one end of the sofa, sipping her coffee. I, at the other end, sipped my evening cup of freshly made espresso, tie lowered, top shirt button unbuttoned, looking forward to a relaxing evening, when boom! It hit. The situation.

It's just so odd—how it all came out of the blue like that. How it all changed so fast. I mean, Sarah and I have known each other since our first year of high school, at Ladue High, and we've been married sixteen years come this June. We were married June 21st, 1987, at precisely 2 p.m. at the Old Cathedral by one of the assistants to the archbishop of . . . and we were engaged for an appropriate year and a half . . . had it all well-planned out . . . God, she was so beautiful that day, that hour-glass shape of hers in that long flowing wedding dress, her long, rich auburn hair, those dark haunting eyes of her . . . she . . . that's why . . . I mean, after fifteen years of . . . it . . . it . . . .

What I am trying to say is that I know my wife—or thought I did. Sure, all married couples have their problems. When we were first married, we had some . . . some "issues" to contend with, but they were all small—small, I tell you. She didn't like some of my ways of . . . and she blamed me for driving away all her closest friends—

which I didn't. They were all low-lives anyway—always wanting to "party." They never gave a thought to their futures or careers. You have to plan in life. You can't go through life . ... I knew something had been bothering her for the last week or so. She'd been quieter and moodier than usual. But she had been ill. My God, the Monday morning two weeks ago, she almost didn't make it to the bathroom. She nearly vomited on our plush white carpet. Can you imagine what vomit would do to a white carpet?

Well, anyway, as I said, it was a shock to me—and all I said was, as *The McNeil/Lehrer Hour* was coming on— and as casually as can be, "Well, let's see what that pathetic, bleeding-heart liberal Kerry says tonight about President Bush. I swear, if Kerry is elected president, he and those other bleeding-heart liberals will ruin the economy of this country."

That's all I said, and she muttered under her breath, and as if she had a splitting headache, "Oh, just give it a rest, will you?"

"Excuse me?" Shocked, I turned to look at her.

As if breaking under the pressure of some tremendous, protracted strain, and with eyes closed, she shook her head from side to side. "I said, 'Why don't you just give it a rest?'"

"What's that mean?"

She didn't respond. She'd been holding one of our black china coffee cups, the ones with the gold filigree rim design, in her small, finely-shaped hands, resting her hands and the cup on her lap. She raised the cup to her pencil-thin rose-colored lips. But, instead of taking a drink, she held the cup there, under her nose. As if trying to warm herself, she breathed in the coffee vapors, which must have been lukewarm by now, at best, and which looked a bit unrefined of her. Then, after taking a sip, she finally said, "Nothing. Just forget it."

After a few moments passed, I asked, "What's wrong, hon? Did you have a bad day at the office?"

"I said," she began, in a voice that was not her usual melodious, soft-spoken voice, "just let it—every day's a bad day for me." The last spewed out with a sudden burst of anger that bordered on hate, and then she added, "Especially around here." Then she turned away, extended her arm and banged the cup down on the matching antique end table, almost breaking the cup and missing the custom-made coaster.

"What's wrong with you?" I asked, dumbfounded, and a bit peeved with her attitude.

She looked me dead straight in the face and said, "You want to know what's wrong with me? I'm sick of it. I'm sick of all of it. Sick of it . . .. It's the same thing, day after day, year after year. Nothing ever changes around here. It's like living in a museum . Everything we do is always planned—look at it from this way, look at it from that way, make a proposal, make a schedule, plan. It's like being a machine, and a human calendar. I am sick of it. I know exactly what I'll be doing Thursday at precisely 9 p.m. twenty years from now—going to bed to get up the next morning at precisely 5 a.m. I'm sick of it. Life is about change, Howard, and nothing ever changes around here."

"Changes?" I asked, confused. "Well, what changes do you want?"

"Anything. Everything," she snapped. "Didn't you ever want to do something that wasn't planned? Do something carefree, on the moment?"

"What are you talking about? Look at last Friday, how I—with no advanced planning—I said, 'Hon, let's go to the symphony.' Huh? What about that? There wasn't any plan—and we didn't even have tickets. Why, we might have gotten there and—"

"Oh, please. The symphony? Boy, you are one free spirit."

"Now, just a minute," I said. "What's this all about? What are you talking about?"

"I'm talking about change!" She nearly screamed it at me. "I'm talking about life. I'm ta—is this all there is? Is this it?" She waved her right hand out towards the room. "Where are we g—"

"I don't understand any of this," I said. "You make it sound like we're standing still. We're moving along. We have our futures planned—in five years the mortgage on the cabin at the lake will be paid off. In ten years you and I will have seventy-five percent of our projected goals of a million each in our financial portfolios. We'll resign from our positions, then open the marketing/advertising agency—which you—"

"There you go again!" she shouted, throwing her arms up in the air. "It's all about money with you. It's all about planning. It's all about being wealthy, being refined, being defined, being right, being, being—being soooo damned precise—and clean. So damn, damn clean! Even your sex is clean!"

"Now, just a damn minute! What in the hell—clean? What does that even mean? What . . . how is my sex cl—"

"Oh, please. You make me change the sheets every time we have sex . . . Thank God, it's only once a week—on Saturday night at precisely ten o'clock. It's disgusting. Disgusting, I tell you. I—I can't take it anymore. I can't. I can't!" She rose from the sofa, turned, took two steps forward, then stopped, as if not knowing where else to go. Then she ripped three or four tissues from the custom-designed tissue box on the end table, and although she had her back to me, I knew she was crying.

"So," I said, "then this is all about me not being any good in bed. I'm not 'dirty' enough for you in bed. You want me to be 'kinky' in—"

She spun and faced me. Through angry tears, she said, "There isn't one thing about you that is 'kinky.' You're too—too predictable for that." She dabbed away tears with the tissues. "You're too—too—too antiseptic for—"

"You take that back!" I shot up off the sofa and faced her. "You take that back. I am not antiseptic."

"Yes, you are."

"Am not."

"Oh, yes you are," she repeated, and then—then—to add salt on an already open wound, she crumbled those tissues into a ball and let it fall on the floor—on our white, plush carpeted floor!—as gracefully as she applies rouge to her soft-skinned, lovely face.

"You pick that up," I demanded, pointing at the tissues.

"No."

"I said, 'Pick that up.'"

"No."

"Well, I am not picking it up."

"Good. Just leave it there."

We stood there, staring at each other while time passed. I looked down at the ball of tissue, then stared at her, growing angrier. She stared back at me, anger in every line of her face, while more time passed.

Finally, I got so angry I felt perspiration tickling down my back, through my shirt and T-shirt. Then I couldn't breathe and my head felt light. That ball of white tissue and the white carpet began to spin, and I exploded. "You're crazy, lady. You've gone mad. You need a psychiatrist. There's something wrong with you." I scooped up the ball of tissue.

Like a volcano about to erupt, she said, "You want to know what's wrong with me? Do you really want to know?"

"Why not? I mean, it's not like I'll be watching my *McNeil/Lehrer Hour*. So, you may as well tell me."

"So you really—really—want to know?"

"Oh, for the love of Christ,' I shouted. "Yes, I want to know. Tell me. Tell me!"

"I'm pregnant!"

A long moment of silence hung between us.

Finally, I said, "I thought you couldn't get—I thought you said a doctor told you years ago because of that time when you were—"

"Well, I did," she said, her voice flat. Looking tired and empty, she sat down on the sofa. "So let's just end this. You go your way and I'll go mine. You never wanted me anyway. All you wanted was a trinket. Someone to pick up your dry cleaning and—"

"Never wanted you?" I asked, shocked. "No, I never wanted you. No, I'm just the guy who adored you from the first moment he saw you. Your faithful, 'platonic' friend all through high school and college—the guy who went to the same college just to be near you.

"No, I'm just the guy who was always there through all of your relationships that went sour . . . jocks, guys with names like Doug and Jim, and—the big jerks. No, I'm just the one—and you knew, you always knew—who begged you to marry him. How shallow a person do you think I am? I resent that. I do . . . I . . . we never talked about kids all these years because it was such a sensitive subject—because of you having. ..."

With a heavy sigh, I returned to my side of the sofa and slumped down on it. I felt something moist in my hand. I opened it and saw the crumpled ball of tissue I'd retrieved from the floor—that ball of tissue wet with her tears. I turned around and, suddenly, that expensive, fashionable, meticulously clean, penthouse apartment seemed different. Dirty, unkempt. I threw the ball of tissue as hard and as far as I could. It hit the west wall, high about the television, bounced off, and came to an unceremonious rest on the plush white carpet.

So, at precisely—no, no more of that 'precisely' crap. Let's just say the *McNeil/Lehrer Hour* had been on for twenty minutes when I looked at her. Feeling more than a little sheepish, I asked, "Do you know the sex of the baby?"

"It's a girl." Joy tinged her voice.

"A girl," I mused. "A baby, wow." I moved closer to her. "I can change, Sarah. I can."

She stood and walked over to the ball of tissue, picked it up, then returned to sit on the sofa, but nearer to me. She looked down at the tissue, then at me.

Placing her left hand on her stomach, she said, "Maybe we both need to change, and should."

After graduating from college here in St. Louis with a B. A. in English, Alan Zacher moved to Los Angeles to become a famous actor. He struggled as an actor for twelve years when he tired of "struggling" and moved back home to St. Louis and turned his hand to writing. He's presently a graduate student at Lindenwood University, in the MFA program for writing.

The Goldfish Tattoo
By Susan Varno

"Sam's dead," Jill said. My secretary looked like she was about to burst into tears.

I rolled my eyes. "No, he's not. He called in 'dead.' That's one step up from calling in 'sick.' I told that kid if he missed one more day of work, I'd fire him no matter who his father is."

"Nora, I don't think this is a joke. A woman called. She was upset."

"He's dating an actress," I said. "Now, he's definitely fired."

My life had been just fine before I hired Sam Reynolds. I ran a successful corporate travel agency. Tom, my attentive boyfriend, didn't pressure me for a commitment, and I was using virtual earplugs to muffle the relentless ticking of my biological clock.

My clients liked Sam, but he wouldn't press for a sale. If he got one, his follow-up was dismal. I kept explaining, encouraging, begging him to follow proper procedure. The boy was bright, charming and creative; but discipline and work ethic were not values he could relate to.

I flipped through my Rolodex for his father's cell phone number. He answered on the first ring.

"Glenn?"

"Yes?"

"This is Nora Landry. I'm calling about Sam. This morning...well, I don't know where to begin. I'm angry, but I want you to understand...."

"Oh, Nora." He sounded as quavery as Jill. "Thank you. I can't believe it either. Can you imagine, killed by a drunk driver at 8:30 in the morning."

My heart climbed into my throat. "On his way to work," I said. On time, I thought. "Is there anything I can do?"

"I don't know," he sighed. "Tell a few people. I'll have someone call you with the arrangements."

Shaking, I hung up, then closed my office door. What do I tell my staff? Sam Reynolds, 23 years old, sparkling brown eyes, disorganized hair and a goofy grin. Lovable Sam with a line of happy chatter and a raucous laugh that made you laugh with him. Sam was gone.

He had a way of getting me to reveal things about myself that were none of his business. Then he'd say something like, "All this advice you give me, you'd make a great mother," or "There's more to life than making money, honey bunny."

Yesterday Sam had said, "Make you a deal. You loosen up and have some fun, and I'll try to do things your way." If he walked through the door right now, I'd agree. All that energy, all love for life, how could he be dead?

I closed the office early so my staff could attend the wake. I dreaded going but stopped by around seven. The funeral home was in a Victorian mansion. The parking lot was full, and police were directing traffic to the side streets.

Inside, the richly paneled rooms were packed body-to-body. The young people looked dazed. These kids believed bullets bounce off them, I thought. Their Sam couldn't be dead.

I worked my way to the guest register, dropped a sympathy card in the slot, and paid my respects to his parents. The coffin was nearly hidden by baskets of flowers. Turning away, I headed for the exit. I didn't want this to be my last memory of Sam.

Outside, the veranda was just as crowded. Someone tapped me on the shoulder. I gritted my teeth and pasted on a smile.

"Are you Miss Landry?" a girl asked.

I nodded, trying to see her features in the fading light.

"I'm Sam's friend Jasie," she said. "He told us about you."

He must have regaled his friends with stories of his uptight boss. "I'm not as bad as he claimed."

"Oh, Sam liked you," she insisted. "Some of his friends want to meet you."

Before I could find an excuse, Jasie introduced me to Sam's high school friends, college friends and people he'd worked with at various jobs. They all loved him.

"There must be two hundred young people here," I said. "They couldn't all have known Sam."

A young man named Kyle said, "Once you were Sam's friend it was forever. He kept in touch with calls, E-mail, parties."

Another young man, I missed his name, shook his head. "Nobody threw a party like Sam."

"He had the best ideas," another young man offered. "Like the time...."

I listened as they shared Sam's party themes. I even offered details of the contest he organized to see which sales associate could make the tallest stack of plastic cups and the afternoon he kept them busy filling the storeroom with blown-up balloons.

Another girl, Corky I think, said, "That's not why we loved him. He took care of us."

Jasie twined her arm through mine. "We're going to a place Sam used to take us when we were down. We're going because...well, you know."

A tall young man took my other arm. "You're coming with us."

"Oh, no," I protested. "Why would you want me to?"

As she moved me down the steps, Jasie said, "Sam always had a project going."

"A project?" Could Sam have been that organized?

The young man who'd been introduced as Paul moved me toward the parking lot. "He'd pick someone, usually someone he'd just met."

Jasie added, "First, he'd turn on the charm, let the person know he liked him or her. Then he'd work on the person's problem. Sam never failed."

I should be digging in my heels and shouting for help, I thought. Sam couldn't have told them to do this because he didn't know he was going to die. But somewhere deep inside, I knew if I didn't go with them I'd always wish I had.

They climbed into an SUV. I was riding "shotgun."

"Were some of you Sam's projects?" I asked. If they planned to "solve my problem," I wanted to know what to expect.

A young woman behind me said, "Sam used to make fun of my looks."

"But, you're...." Even in the dark, I could see she was lovely.

Paul added, "She used to look like every day was Halloween—black make-up, leather and chains, piercings. Didn't you have green hair?"

"Purple," she said. "Then one day Sam threw a hose party."

I had to ask. "A what?"

"You know, garden hose, back yard, sneak up on people as they arrive. Anyway, he washed my make-up off. Then he pretended he didn't know who I was. He started coming on to me." She started to cry. "Sam let me know I was hiding behind all that junk."

Others told how Sam had bailed them out of jail, covered for them when they were in trouble, lent them money, clothes or his car. He fixed the shy ones up with the friendly ones and kept others from driving drunk. A few mentioned drugs, abusive relationships, bad home situations.

One young man insisted, "I was never one of Sam's projects."

The others hooted. "Since when?"

He frowned.

"You and girls," they said in unison.

"Oh, yeah. I guess." He grinned. He seemed okay with girls now.

Paul drove to the edge of town. Turning off the headlights, he eased the van down a gravel road. He parked behind some bushes, and we all got out. Kyle pulled back a loose section of chain link fence. One by one, we ducked under.

Suddenly, they were running, pulling me across several sets of train tracks. If a train was coming, I couldn't have heard it over the roar of crickets. Where are we going? I wondered as they led me through bushes and tall weeds. Broken bottles and unknown debris crunched underfoot.

We came out by the abandoned bottling plant. The three-story brick building was completely dark—no lights inside or out. The tallest boy leaped up and grabbed the end of the fire escape; the other boys pulled on his feet until the ladder creaked to the ground. This had to be dangerous, I thought, not to mention illegal. If we got caught, my name would be in the newspaper. But I'd come this far, not to mention I was leery of walking by myself back the way we came.

We climbed thirty or so feet to the roof. Raised skylights broke up the flat-tarred surface. People in movies were always falling through skylights. What am I doing here? But the view was spectacular. The lights of town sparkled in the distance; the sky was dark enough to see the stars. The young people made a circle around the largest skylight.

"Now what?" I whispered to Jasie.

"We remember Sam."

I remembered Sam. How he irritated me, how I was sure he'd never amount to anything, how I was sorry I'd hired him. How I missed him. How quiet the office was without him. And how boring.

Some of the girls were crying. The boys put their arms around them. I couldn't expect anyone to offer me comfort, but I needed someone to hold me. Then everybody started hugging everybody, including me. I didn't cry. Not yet.

"We have to sing his song," Jasie said.

They broke out with all the verses of "Friends." I only knew the chorus, "I'll be there for you like I've been there before." Singing included some dance moves. I couldn't help myself, I swayed a little.

"This is way too sad," someone said.

"If Sam was here, he'd come up with a great idea," someone else said.

"We have to do something so we don't forget him."

"We'll never forget him. But like what?"

Jasie said, "We should all get the same tattoo. Sam wanted one. Remember, he went to the tattoo parlor; but somebody talked him out of it." They all glared at the former "black make-up" girl.

"All I did was talk him out of a full back tattoo," she said.

"A heart with 'We love you, Sam'," called another voice in the dark.

Jasie said. "How will we girls explain that to our boyfriends and future husbands?"

"Dilbert," I said. I glanced around to make sure the word had come out of my mouth.

"Who?" asked several people.

"Sam's goldfish," I explained. "He kept it on his desk. Told me it was a 'babe magnet.' I've been taking care of it." At least I would as soon as I got back to the office. How long can a goldfish go without food? I wondered. "Something small and tasteful," I added. "A goldfish tattoo."

"Like where? I mean should we all put the goldfish in the same place?"

They discussed various body parts including a few I considered inappropriate. In the end, they decided we'd each chose our own location.

Jasie said, "Tomorrow, we'll go to the tattoo parlor together. Right after the funeral." She turned to me. "You're coming, aren't you?"

I paused. "If I'm not there, start without me."

I got home at midnight after stopping by the office to feed Dilbert. He'd looked grateful as he gobbled fish flakes.

Flipping on the light, I wondered what Sam would say about my apartment. Great view, color coordinated—what my interior designer called "continuity." Sam would say it looked like it oozed off of the "Fine Living" channel. No clutter, nothing out of place, like no one lives here. Not even me, I thought.

I still needed a good cry; but like the kid said, this was way too sad.

One message blinked on my answering machine. I pushed the button, wanting to hear a human voice even if it was a telemarketer.

"Nora, it's me, Tom. Haven't been in touch for a few days. Call me."

He'd be asleep, but I dialed his home number. His answering machine picked up. What did I want to say? I love you. Let's get married. I want to have a son and name him Sam.

His outgoing message finished. I stood for a few seconds with the phone in my hand. "I'm getting a tattoo tomorrow," I said softly and hung up.

The phone rang. I jumped. "Caller ID" said it was Tom. I was going to cry. I'd be embarrassed, he'd be upset. I should let it ring.

I picked up the phone.

"A tattoo?" he said. "What's the joke?"

"No joke. I'm really getting a tattoo. A goldfish. I promised some people."

"Nora...." His tone changed. "Are you serious?"

I was definitely going to cry. "Remember I told you about Sam Reynolds?"

"The kid who drives you crazy at the office? What's he done now?"

"He died," I said.

Susan Varno's published writing includes over 100 articles about the Ozarks in regional magazines and local newspapers. She writes feature articles for the *Three Rivers Edition* of the *Arkansas Democrat Gazette* and two monthly columns for *Video Views Magazine*. Twenty-two of her short stories have been published, most in confession magazines.

The Good Lord Giveth
By Dusty Richards

The smell of wood smoke in the air made me spur my horse, Bronc, up on the mesa to find the source. I was heading home after helping an old friend put up a shed. Once on top, I saw a single teepee and a woman in wind-swept buckskin fringe bent over tending a fire. Three paint horses raised their heads and nickered at Bronc. I looked over the situation and sent him off in a running walk toward her camp. Maybe I could buy a meal. The jerky in my saddle bags was getting where it tasted plain monotonous.

Where was her man? No telling. I guessed her to be a Cheyenne or Arapahoe. She glanced up at my approach and then went back to tending her cooking. Not a short woman by any means, she stood close to six feet tall. In her twenties, I guessed, and she reminded me of a willow tree in the wind.

When I got close, she raised to her full height and nodded. I saw half of her face was painted with charcoal. Right down through her slender nose, the left side was black. All I could figure was she must be a widow.

I held up my hand in a peace sign and she nodded. After a check around to be certain this was no trap, I dismounted. Dropped the reins—Bronc wouldn't run off. He was ground-tie broke. Out of habit, I hitched up my pants and adjusted my gun belt before I walked over to her.

Hat in hand, I said, "My name is Nick Carter. Do you speak English?"

"I speak English very well, Nick Carter."

"I see you do. What are you cooking?"

"Deer meat."

"Could I buy a meal from you?"

"No."

"Fine." I started to turn back to my horse.

"No, I mean I will feed you. I need none of your money."

"Mighty generous of you, ma'am." I set my hat back on my head. The afternoon wind was stirring up good out of the south. I loosened the cinch some on my saddle and then rejoined her at the fire. I didn't really need the heat, the sun was high, but I squatted down on my boot heels. Coming to a person's fire shows you're friendly. I sure had no quarrel with this woman and especially since she was generous enough to feed me—plus, aside from that black paint, she was a damn good looking woman. Oh, a little tall, but I couldn't hold that against her either.

"I am in mourning," she said.

"I'm so sorry for you. I figured you were, that black paint on your face and all."

"My man was White Elk. A white man shot him."

"What for?"

"He said he stole a cow."

"Did he?"

She shook her head, and then tied her long, clean-looking hair back with a piece of fringe she cut off her sleeve. "No."

"Who was this man who shot him?"

"I don't know. But he is dead now, too."

At that moment I wasn't certain I wanted to know who killed the man, but I asked, "Did you kill him?"

She nodded. "White Elk never took anything from that man. His killer was drunk at the time too."

"Guess he deserved killing."

She never made any sign, yes or no, merely spooned out a tin plate full of steaming meat and handed it to me. I looked it over and nodded my approval. "Thank you."

"You can say a white man's prayer over it?" Then she bowed her head in anticipation.

"Lordy, lady, what's your name?"

"My name in Cheyenne is Blue Flower."

"Oh, alright, Blue. I'll think of a prayer." Heavens, I hadn't said a prayer in years. Maybe at Bucky's funeral, but this wasn't a funeral, not for anyone I knew.

"Lord, we're out here under your skies today. We'd like you to bless this food so it nourishes our body. Help Blue get over the loss of her good man and be in our hearts when we separate—amen."

She raised her head and opened her brown eyes. "Good prayer. My food didn't even get cold."

I nodded, grinned, and tried the first bite. The stew tasted good and drew the saliva in my mouth. Busy eating the rich stew, I about forgot my manners. "Ma'am, these are really find vittles. Good nourishment for an old cowboy."

"What does 'nourish' mean?"

"Means it'll make you strong." I was surprised I had her an answer. Living out on the northern plains by myself so long, I'd forgotten most of my manners or even how to speak to civilized folks.

"Good prayer you give us."

"Well, Blue, I ain't no preacher. Matter of fact . . .." I was at a loss for words that I wanted to tell her. Some forty-year-old who got drunk every time I went to town. Cussed like a sailor and visited the parlor houses when I saw one open.

"You have a family?" she asked.

"No. Never been married."

"You have a home?"

"Yes, a damn good one. It's warm in winter and dry."

She nodded she heard me. "Where is your place?"

"Up on Cherry Creek, north of here, at the crossing. You know where that is?"

Seated cross-legged beside me, she took my empty plate and refilled it. "I think I know."

"Come by. I'll feed you. You know NC. I got that brand on my things. Thanks, these are mighty good vittles." I accepted the second steaming plate from her.

"Maybe I'll do that—some time. Come see you. Your vest is torn. I can sew it."

"I guess it will be in shreds soon, if I don't let you." She smiled.

The afternoon flew by. She mended my vest. I fixed the girth on her pack saddle and went over the rest of her gear. Most of her horse rigging was substantial enough. Don't know what got into me. Ordinarily, I'd of had the sugar foot so bad by this time I'd be half-way home. But she was a peaceful woman to be around, aside from that half-black face that still shocked me when she turned toward me.

We talked some about my Texas cows and the new shorthorn bulls I bought last fall. I told her about the fancy wood cook stove I got from some folks moving west who needed some money.

In the late afternoon, when we feasted on some more of her deer stew, it was clouding up in the south. Where had the time gone? I felt more settled than I had in years, just sitting and talking with her. It was past time for me to head for home in the daylight, but I had a canvas sheet and a blanket behind my cantle cause I got caught out lots of nights.

After supper, we took Bronc and her horses down on the creek and watered them. I was impressed how she hopped on her horse, then whistled for the other two and they came along. She could damn sure ride as well. That hillside going up and down off that mesa was steep, and she clung like a tick to her pony's back. Once back to her teepee, I unsaddled Bronc and hobbled him. She undid my bedroll and then shouldered my saddle.

"Where're you going?" I asked.

"Rains coming. No need for your saddle to get wet. I can store it in my house."

"Thanks. I'll go kick me out a place to sleep out here."

"My home has plenty of room."

"Naw, I'll sleep out here. Thank you, anyway."

Before I shut my eyes, I heard the way-off first rumble of thunder. The storm probably wouldn't get up that far. Besides, in the summer time, most rains shut off after sundown. I was set under my canvas wrap and closed my eyes.

When I awoke, thunder cracked overhead like Fourth of July fireworks. In the next flash of lightning, I saw her wrapped in a blanket and trying to wake me.

"Bad storm. You come with me quick."

I gathered up everything and followed her outline toward the teepee. Every time lightning flashed, I could see her form and the flapping blanket, until I threw in the bedroll and crawled on my knees inside her teepee. I straightened and the hail began beating on the hide walls. The noise was hellacious and I wondered how the tall structure would stand the whistling wind and battering storm without toppling over.

When it let up some, I looked around her house in the flickering light of the one small candle she had lit. "I think the worst is over."

She agreed and, since my blankets were wet, told me to join her. I fought off my boots, then put them and my gun belt in a pile with my hat. Her pallet was a large pile of blankets and furs. I lifted the edges to get in and aimed to be on the outer edge of the bed. She had her back to me.

And that was fine.

"You better say a prayer to your God for saving us," she said over the rain's gentle drumming.

"I will. I will. Dear God, thanks for delivering Blue and I from that storm out here. Keep us in your palm and safe as we sleep. Amen."

"Amen. Good," she said.

That thunder grew louder and then further away. Lying there in my clothes, I could smell her scent like the fragrance of flowers and listened to the storm until my eyes fell shut. When my hand felt her silky bare skin, I nearly set right up in bed. I sure didn't want to wake her, but she was plumb naked and sound asleep. Quick as I could, I rolled over on my other side and turned my back to her.

Next thing I knew, she was up against me with an arm slung over me. I never moved.

When I woke the next time, the sun had came up and she wasn't in the bed. Outside, I could hear her making a fire. Bleary-eyed, I pulled on my boots and strapped on my gun. Since I'd been gone five days, I decided I better get on back to the ranch. Her half-black face and all the rest of her had me about shook. Not that she wasn't nice, but I had a bad case of the *bejeepers* being near her and sure wanted to be on my way.

We ate the rest of her stew, talked about the good rain and everything. Then she went for my saddle and I went for Bronc. She straightened the pad on his back, then swung the kak in place. She wouldn't let me do anything, and when she finished she turned and smiled at me.

"Now you may leave, after you pray for both of us."

My, my, she sure was into this prayer business. She had me down on my knees beside her. "Dear God. As we part this morning, let Blue find some peace in her life and relieve her of the burden of her lost husband and let her get on with her life. Thanks for the rain and the wind and see us safely on our way. Amen."

She caught my arm and held me there. "You're a fine man, Nick Carter. May God ride with you, too."

"Thank you, Blue. If you get hungry or lost come on up to my ranch."

She nodded that she heard me.

I looked into her half and half face. "God bless you, girl."

Then I left her. I wasn't quite sure why. Neither of us had anyone nor a helluva lot to do. When I looked back, she waved. At that point, I about turned Bronc around, but decided not to. She needed to get clear of her late husband and the memories of him. I had no right to confuse her with my needs—they were all the gut needs of a man.

A week went by. I busied myself building a pole corral addition, then rode to the north end of my range to turn some other stock away and drift some of mine back. I'd been gone several days, when I returned and saw the teepee first—set up fifty yards from the house. My heart began to pound. Worn out from all the riding I'd done, as well as sleeping on the hard ground a couple of nights. The notion she'd come to see me lifted a heavy yoke off my neck.

I rode up to her teepee and she came out in a white elk dress. The black paint was gone from her face and she rushed toward me. Dismounted, I rushed to hug her and swing her around. Had she come to join me?

I damn sure didn't know, but my heart raced and my breath was short just thinking about having her company. Every muscle in my body trembled, inside and out, as I hugged her firm body to mine. I simply could not get enough of her pressed to me. Then, whiskers and all, I kissed her on the mouth.

She blinked her eyes and hugged me tighter. "I like that."

"Tell you, I like that, too. But why you came here?"

"For this. Nick Carter, you are a good man. I am a simple Cheyenne woman who no longer cries for her man. I came to share my life with you, if you will have me."

"Wouldn't you rather find one of your own? And I must be twice your age."

With the sides of her fists, she beat me on the chest. "You aren't that old and you have a big heart inside you."

What could I do? I never thought I needed a bride, let alone an Indian woman. But she was not an Indian woman, she was a spirit who came on the wind and storm to me. From the same God who gave me the rain, he sent her.

"Do you want me to stay?" she asked.

"Lord, yes, girl. You have been in my dreams every night since I met you and I even saw you in those shafts of light coming through the clouds."

She dropped on her knees and pulled me down. "Then pray to your God for us to never part."

"Lord, I am asking . . .."

That was ten years ago, and Blue and I have two children, Little Nick and Flora. I bought several homesteaders out and my ranch has doubled in size since then. The NC brand is on a lot more cattle.

The neighbors and us have a little church we all built over on Bug Creek where we belong. On Sundays, we all sing hymns and pray, cause I'm a grateful man for him sending me such a beautiful woman for my wife and for showing me a way to the Lord. Amen.

Dusty Richards won two Spur Awards in 2007. One for his novel, *The Horse Creek Incident*, and one for *Comanche Moon*, a short story. Dusty was honored again in April of 2010 when the National Cowboy & Western Heritage Museum gave their annual Heritage Award to his novel, *Sundown Chaser*. Dusty and his wife, Pat, reside next to Beaver Lake east of Springdale, Arkansas—that is when they aren't off at speaking engagements or writing conferences, announcing rodeos or chuck wagon racing, or researching for western novels.

The Red Quilt
By Georgia Alderink

The rides, the tinny music, the shills shouting, the animals: I can see, hear and smell the county fair yet. But most of all I remember the quilt exhibition hall.

"Look, but don't touch," my mother would say as my fingers itched to rub the quilts, to feel the textures. I'd marvel at the small pieces, the tiny stitches, then step back and admire the colors and patterns. It piqued a desire to learn quilting.

By the time I met and married Bob I had mastered the basics and turned out beautiful, traditional quilts. As a photographer, Bob had a keen eye for color and form and he encouraged me to experiment.

"The old patterns are beautiful, Jo," he would say, "but you're an artist—use your ability." Tentatively I let myself try new things and learned to enjoy my creativity. I discovered I could create pictures within the quilt, sometimes using the traditional quilt patterns as borders and sometimes making the quilt entirely my own design. Embroidery and beads added depth and interest. Now museums display my creations and my time is spent creating and teaching.

Our home is spacious and light-filled. We built it not only as a home but as a showcase for my quilts and a schoolroom for aspiring artists. My studio fills our home's second floor, my husband's photography studio is a stone's throw away, connected to the house by a walkway. The walkway is a physical connection between us during the day, but there is another connection; his talent and charismatic personality. Our talents, though expressed differently, are linked and I get inspiration and energy through this link. Could I create without him? Are my quilts all crafted with an eye to his praise?

This morning I sit here doodling and thinking. The design for an underwater scene, a Baltimore aquarium commission, niggles at my mind. If I pay attention, I can see part of the photography studio parking lot from my workplace. Today as I gaze out the window thinking of oceans and fish and seaweed, I notice a white car drive in. A tall, thin brunette slams the car door shut and heads for the photography entrance.

"That's odd," I say to myself. "It's the third or fourth time I've noticed her. She must be a model. Either Bob's having a problem photographing her or she's given him a large assignment." I turn back to my doodling and musing but the picture of the beautiful brunette stays in my mind.

It seems like minutes later that my stomach tells me it's time to prepare dinner and I head downstairs, my mind still on the new design coming to life under my fingers. Leftovers for dinner tonight, I think. Quick and easy. Yesterday I prepared a meal for twenty people. Tours come often. I prepare a meal, talk about quilting and earn a good sum. We all enjoy it and I believe they get their money's worth.

"Hey Bob," I call into the intercom. "Time to eat." The sound of the side door closing comes seconds before my husband bounds into the kitchen. He's a tall man, graying, as I am, but in better shape. He spends nearly as many hours at his photography as I do at my quilting, but also takes time to work out. When we can, we enjoy hiking together, but I know I should spend more time exercising.

Age is creeping up.

"Yo, Jo," he says and looks me over. For some reason I'm uncomfortable under his scrutiny and think of the brunette. I pull in my stomach and smooth my hair.

Mealtimes are our visiting times, our "catch up with each other" times, but today Bob seems distracted, almost vibrating with a nervous energy. My attempts at conversation reach dead ends and it puzzles me. Finally I ask him, "Who's the brunette, Bob?"

"The brunette?"

"Yes, I've noticed a white car with a brunette at the wheel several times, and I wonder who she is. Is she giving you a large assignment?"

"The brunette? Oh, you must mean Jean. Jean McDonald. I've been making a folio for her. She wants to get into modeling. She's been by a couple of times."

"She looks like a model. Beautiful girl."

"Yes, I guess so. Photographs well." Bob runs his fingers through his thick hair. "What have you been working so busily on lately?"

"The underwater scene for Baltimore. It's coming along well," I answer. My mind registers the fact he's changing the subject. Is it deliberate?

"I'm looking forward to our Minneapolis trip Friday," I say. "Jan Patek and Barb and Alma Adams will be showing quilts and lecturing. I see the Ansel Adams exhibit is at the Minneapolis Institute of Art now. We'll both enjoy that."

"I've almost forgotten about the trip, I've been so busy. But it'll be fun I guess."

"You don't sound very enthusiastic."

"Just stressed, Jo."

I get up to clear the table. Why do I feel so edgy?

Days go by fast as I'm immersed in my new quilt. I've selected the materials I need for the seaweed and the tropical fish. It always excites me—this waiting to see just how my design will turn out. As I sew today I look out the window and again notice the white car with the brunette at the wheel.

"Why does she make you nervous?" I ask myself as I watch her stride toward the door. "Bob sees all kinds of beautiful women. You've never had a problem with that." But I *am* having a problem and find myself going to the window every time I hear a car door slam.

For several days I force myself to ignore the slamming of car doors outside my window. "Don't borrow trouble," I say to myself. "Bob loves me. I know that." But depression lurks beneath the surface and even the iridescent fish swimming under the needle of my sewing machine don't help me shake it off.

Today, a sixth sense tells me Jean is in the studio. I look out the window and don't see the white car, but I know she's there. I fight with myself. Bob's workplace has always been off-limits to me when he's working, just as mine has been to him. Our jobs need our concentration. Should I go over? What excuse can I give? What if she's there? What if she isn't there? Finally some inward need I am not able to deny makes me put down my sewing and go.

I walk slowly, hating myself for doing this. My mind hardly registers the beautiful day. My stomach jumps and I rub my hands over my arms as though it were cold outside. I hear a woman's voice and pause. Just as I reach for the doorknob, Jean opens the door, nearly hitting me. She stops, a stunned expression on her face. "Excuse me," she stammers, "I didn't know you were there."

"No I don't suppose you would have," I say. We look at each other. I see her, dark hair caught up in a loose chignon, a filmy blouse over her breasts and long legs loosely covered in a wonderful shade of green silk. Without touching, my fingers can feel the material's smoothness and I clench my hands. Dark brown eyes look at me, then drop. She is truly lovely. My courage falters. I back away, turn, and go quickly to the house.

"What's wrong, Jo? You've been looking as though you've lost your best friend," Bob asks that evening as we relax in front of the fireplace.

"Nothing's wrong," I say quickly.

He sits on the floor, slippered feet toward the fire, his red, plaid flannel shirt open at the neck, jeans hugging his legs. I love him. I love the look of him. I love the feel of him. I also know tonight he is not as relaxed as he appears. There is again that aura of what? Nervousness? Tension? Agitation? He reads the paper, but it is obvious he is not actually reading—he turns the pages, sets it down, picks it up, turns the pages again.

"About the Minneapolis trip," he says, setting the paper down again. "I really don't think I should go, Jo."

"Not go? You've been looking forward to it almost as much as I have. Why not?"

"Work has been coming in faster than I can take care of it."

"You need some time off. The work will still be here. It's just a four-day trip."

"I don't feel comfortable about it now. You go and have a good time."

My eyes leave his face and focus on the fire. Finally I look back and say impulsively, "Bob, are you having an affair with Jean?"

Bob gets to his feet and stands over me.

"An affair? With Jean? Are you out of your mind? I'm an old married man—Jean's a beautiful young woman. She wouldn't have an affair with me even if I tried to seduce her. Which I haven't." His voice softens as he looks at me and continues. "We've been married a long time, Jo. I love you—always have, always will."

Tears come to my eyes. I want to believe him.

I nearly cancel the trip. Visions of Bob and Jean play through my head and I imagine the worst. But, in spite of my fears, the trip goes well. The city has always fascinated me, and an old friend, Ellen Anderson, and I explore old haunts and discover new. We go to the Ansel Adams exhibit and I find I enjoy it even without Bob. As we eat salad at the Olive Garden restaurant we discuss the quilters and the new things we have seen. Then it is time to go home.

As I pull into our driveway I notice Bob's car is not in the garage. I park and sit, irresolute. Shall I go in the house, or should I check out his studio?

"Don't be an ass, Jo," I tell myself. "What do you think you'd find in his studio? Incriminating evidence?"

Setting common sense aside, I take out his studio key and unlock the door. The pungent odor of developing fluid greets me and I enter cautiously, almost as though I expect to see Bob and Jean intertwined on the floor. Pictures line the walls. Pictures of babies, Ozark scenery pictures that I recognize from our hikes, pictures of graduates, and glamour shots of young women. And pictures of Jean. Many pictures of Jean. I stare, transfixed.

The artist loved his subject. He could not have taken these pictures otherwise. I turn quickly as I hear a step behind me.

"You *are* home," he says, leaning against the door. "I saw your car. Did you have a good trip?"

"You love her, don't you?" I ask as I turn to again stare at the pictures.

"I love all my subjects when I'm photographing them. That's why I'm good. Come into the house, Jo. I brought takeout from Madame Wu's for our dinner."

"Bob," I say over the breakfast table a week later.

He grunts, reading the sport section of the <u>Democrat Gazette</u>. "What'd you say?"

"How about taking the day off tomorrow and hiking the Goat Trail? We haven't been there in a long time."

Bob sets down the paper and stirs his coffee, obviously thinking. "I guess I could. There's nothing going on that I can't put off for a day."

The hike from the highway to the Goat Trail is the longest part, and I chatter aimlessly as we walk along. Bob is pleasant but quiet. Several times I notice him staring out into space, an expression on his face I can't define. We come to the trail's narrow ledge and stand. The Buffalo River snakes through the valley far below. We shade our eyes against the brightness as we watch a hawk play with the air currents. The current lifts the bird high, and then drops him. The hawk circles aimlessly as he waits for the next current, like a surfer waiting for a wave. As I watch, my stomach contracts, like I myself am one with the hawk, flying and falling.

Bob puts his arm around me and we sit, resting our backs against the bluff. "That hawk is enjoying life, isn't he. Going with the flow, not worrying about tomorrow." He turns his head and gazes down the river. "This place is beyond description," he says. "How many photographs have I shot here and not one does it justice."

A few days later I find the note. I pull it out of Bob's pocket and know what it is before I read it. My breath comes fast and my legs are weak. I force myself to sit, to calm down. "Don't open it," my brain screams. Then, just as loudly it shrills, "Go ahead, open it. Find out. Not knowing is killing you."

I open the paper and read, "Bob, it was the best. When can we be together again? J." I crumple the paper, recognizing the White Diamonds scent, and toss it in the wastebasket. Then I retrieve it, smoothing it and reading it repeatedly. So, my instincts were right. I grimace. What a clichè. Wife goes through husband's pockets before taking them to the cleaners. Wife finds note. Wife is devastated.

Life continues. I go through the motions. The brightly colored underwater scene gets thrown in a heap and I find myself picking out reds. Bright reds, dull reds, patterned reds and plain reds. I piece the reds into the traditional wedding ring pattern but break the rings. Engrossed in my sewing, I lose track of time.

"Jo," Bob says from the doorway. I jump, startled.

"What are you doing, Jo? I've hardly seen you for days."

"Go, Bob. Leave me alone. Go to your lover."

"What do you mean?"

"You know what I mean. You never have learned to check your pockets. I found a note. Jean wasn't setting up a photography appointment."

Bob stares at me and I meet his gaze defiantly. His hands reach toward me, then drop.

"She means nothing to me. You're my wife. I'm not leaving you."

I turn to face him, pieces of red material in my hands. "I'm not your wife any longer. Not now. Leave me alone. Go."

He comes closer and looks directly into my face.

"Jo, I, ... you don't understand."

"You're right. I don't understand. Not your unfaithfulness. All I understand is that I want you to leave." I raise my voice. "I don't you want you around here, Bob."

He turns, face pale, shoulders slumped.

I hear him in the bedroom and know he is packing. I stand still for a moment, then go back to work.

Finally I go to the hall closet and take out my wedding dress. Carefully I cut out pieces here and there, a bit of lace, some beadwork. I work these whites into the reds. There are some red, tear-shaped glass beads in my "everything" jar. I sew them nearly in the middle of the piece—red tears within the white.

Days later, finished, I take the hanging downstairs and clamp it on the quilt holders. Like paintings, my creations can be appreciated better from a distance, so I walk across the room. As I turn, the intensity of the quilt engulfs me. The anger and humiliation sewed into the piece make it both terrible and beautiful. I hear a noise at the door. Bob stands and stares at the red quilt, then walks over to read the title. "Heartbreak, 2002, Jo Brighton," he reads aloud from the tiny embroidered stitches in the corner.

"Your work is magnificent, Jo. I'm sorry I was the cause."

"Is that all you can say, that you're sorry?" My voice is cold. "All these years of marriage and you've thrown them down the drain. I loved you. I've loved you since I was seventeen." I drop down on the couch, and hold my hands over my face, not wanting him to see what jealousy and anger look like.

Bob sits beside me and starts to put his arm around my shoulders. I shake it off.

"Jo, hon, let me come back. Please let me come ... I didn't mean it to happen, and it won't happen again."

"Don't tell me that. Don't tell me you didn't mean to." Even to my ears my voice sounds clipped and hard.

"I want to come home, Jo."

"Why? Is she through with you?"

Then, in my mind's eye I see a young girl, braids hanging down her back. She's looking at quilts. I hear Mother say, "Look, but don't touch." Is that what it felt like for him, the desire to touch, to do the prohibited?

My voice softens and I say, "Look at that quilt, Bob. I didn't know if I could work without you. I'm glad I can. But now I want some time. Just give me some time. Please."

Bob stands and looks at me, "Okay. I'll keep in touch, Jo." He gazes at the quilt for a long minute. "It's the best thing you've ever done. It truly is magnificent."

Georgia Alderink lives with her husband in Fayetteville, Arkansas. Her first middle grade reader was published in 2005. Her second children's book, *Peabrain and Wheelchair Willie*, was published in 2009.

Bonds of Matrimony
By M. Carolyn Steele

"*N*obody exceptin' you and God know 'bout this. It better stay that way."

The threat rumbled out of Rufus' mouth and I knew he meant every word 'cause he fixed me with his squinty eye. It surprised me, I can tell you that. I didn't know Rufus had much truck with the Almighty.

"This seems a mite silly, Rufus. Don't you suppose folks'll notice you're trussed up like a Christmas turkey?" As soon as I said it, I was sorry and took a step back just to be safe.

At first it didn't seem Rufus heard me. He just kept tugging at his coat 'til he managed to fasten one button and the strain on that poor little thing was considerable.

"Not if'n you keep your trap shut. I aim to catch the eye of one of them cherry blossoms." His voice was unnatural deep, like he couldn't get enough air. "I drew first lot and I don't aim to be late." He brushed his hat all around, settled it on his head, and slammed out the cabin door with me taggin' along behind.

I have to admit Rufus cut quite a figure stomping down the trail to town. He reached up and yanked loose a sprig of knobnolly pine and rubbed it on both cheeks. Said Madam Trusseau's girls like fresh-smellin' men, so he reckoned them mail-order brides comin' in on the stage from Kansas City might do the same. I took note of such, 'cause I get a turn at the next shipment of ladies lookin' to be wed.

More'n once Rufus stopped to catch his breath and near turned blue in the face. He'd clutch his belly like it might explode and I feared it would. Then where'd I be? Minus a partner, I can tell you that and I don't envy workin' that sorry ol' mine by myself, all on account o' Rufus' vanity.

I was powerful relieved when that stagecoach come in sight and reined to a stop in front of the trading post 'cause I didn't think Rufus could stand it much longer.

As soon as the dust settled, an angel with red hair springing from under her bonnet stepped down and looked straight at Rufus. She 'bout took my breath away, I can tell you that much, and I worried the same for my ol' partner.

"Oh, Lordy." Rufus gasped, 'cause by now he could barely offer his arm. "I got first draw and I reckon you're mine." This time his voice was unnatural high and his squinty eye went to flutterin'.

The redhead giggled and fanned herself even though there was a right pert wind kickin' up. "I reckon so," she said and held out one hand.

"Ask her, Rufus, can she cook? I'm powerful tired of beans." I aim to be gettin' somethin' out of this deal if'n I'm givin' up my share of the bed and sleepin' out to the shed with nothin' but spiders and such for company.

"Don't mind my partner. He ain't never had no company manners." Rufus give me a shove.

I considered shoving back 'til I recollected his constraints and figured it wouldn't be a fair fight. I surely do wish I could be a fly on the wall of McBurney's boarding house come nightfall. I'd like to see the look on that redhead's face when Rufus shucks them clothes and can't get out of Madam Trusseau's corset by hisself. Don't reckon he thought of that.

Yes, sir. I imagine even the Almighty will have a good laugh then.

M. Carolyn Steele has won numerous writing awards and has short stories published in several anthologies. She combines her knowledge of writing and genealogy to present programs on recording ancestor stories and is the author of the book, *Preserving Family Legends for Future Generations*. Carolyn won Voices Award for Fiction in 2009 and was nominated for a Pushcart Prize.

Hide and Seek
By Velda Brotherton

$\mathcal{T}$he bus entered Galveston along the wide highway. Flashes of sunlight strobed through spreading tree branches, mocking Rana's vision. In a grassy yard a little girl tumbled and played with a puppy. A woman appeared on the verandah, held out both arms. Squealing with delight, the child skipped across the lawn, puppy at her heels, raced up the steps and into the woman's arms. Rana cried out. Caught in her mother's embrace. Planting a kiss on that rose red mouth. The illusion overpowered her and she swallowed a painful knot. Tears poured down her cheeks.

What was going on? That couldn't have been a memory, yet her heart told her it had happened. How odd, because she'd never been in Galveston in her entire life, in fact never been in the United States until this week. What was she remembering? And why?

She shook her head and leaned back against the seat. She'd probably fallen asleep, had a dream. But it'd been so real she'd smelled the grass and the sea breezes.

At the hotel she showered, slipped into black tailored pants, white blouse, black blazer and three inch heels, picked up her slim handbag and heavy briefcase and headed downstairs. Chocolate confections were everywhere for this, the first of a four-day world-wide conference in which companies like her parents' would exhibit their sweet, yummy products.

On the elevator she glanced up to find bright blue eyes openly studying her. His name tag read Logan Carnes and he smiled and nodded. Such a handsome man deserved more than a casual look.

"Hello, Mr. Carnes. How are you enjoying the conference so far?"

"Well, it's a conference. By the way, I'm Logan to the ladies . . . Rana." His dimples popped.

Good Lord, she could go for him in a big way. "And just how do you know my name?"

"Noticed your name tag."

She joined his soft chuckle. "And how do you know I'm a lady?"

"By the cut of your clothes, my dear. Could I buy you a drink before the evening festivities begin?"

Rather than answer, she asked, "Are you in chocolate?"

He glanced down at his western shirt and tight jeans, stopping at the tips of shiny black boots. "I don't think so. Is that a requisite to joining me for a drink?"

For the first time in her life, Rana found herself tongue tied in front of a man. "It's just that . . . I mean . . ." She gave up explaining. "I'd enjoy having a drink with you, Logan."

His craggy good looks and pleasant voice with its Texas drawl plucked gently at her heartstrings.

Before he could say more the elevator stopped on the ground level and he held back to let her off. Momentarily confused as to which way to go, she hesitated long enough for him to take her elbow gently and guide her to the right and into a small, dark bar.

Over Mojitas they exchanged bits and pieces of their lives. The occasional haunted look behind the sparkle in his eyes hinted that he surely hid as many secrets as she did. That didn't matter. Not yet.

"I run a security business out of Austin called Ride Herd. We help small companies protect their businesses and employees, and that's why I'm here. So no, I'm not 'in chocolate.' I could use a little more business from those who are, though."

"Ride Heard?"

"Yeah, you know, ride herd. Cattle drives? Stampeding cattle? Clint Eastwood?"

She choked on her drink, patted her lips with a napkin and studied him. "You're serious?"

"Of course, I'm always serious." His hand on hers, thumb rubbing gently over her skin sent a shiver down her spine.

"I doubt that very much, uh, Logan."

"How about you?"

"I'm never serious."

"No, I mean, where are you in chocolate at?"

"Oh, Switzerland. My parents own a small company there, and they sent me here in the hopes we could pick up some new American contacts."

"Switzerland, huh? Never been there, but I might go." He continued to hold her hand and she let him.

As the conference progressed, she and Logan grew comfortable together. He grabbed every chance to sit beside her at the company sponsored meals and presentations.

On the third day, they were scheduled to take a tour of some of the lovely Victorian homes in Galveston, and he had a seat saved for her when she climbed on the bus.

Each night since arriving, she had dreamed of the child and the Victorian house, but they were peaceful dreams reaching out to embrace her with warmth. She began to welcome them. In those dreams the woman who was her mother did something her own mother never had, and that was to hug and kiss her. Her parents always took good care of her, but she'd never felt that kind of love. They were as cold as their country, a place she'd never belonged.

The tour bus stopped at the curb and she glanced out the window to see the house. A sign in the yard read: NORTHRIDGE HOUSE HISTORICAL LANDMARK. Open Tuesday through Sunday 10 a.m. to 4 p.m. Hosted by the Galveston Historical Society.

This was the house that had sparked her visions, the one she visited in her dreams each night since arriving. This was her home. She felt it in her bones like the lingering spirit of a loved one. Fellow tour passengers rose and filed out of the bus, and still she sat staring through the glass.

"You okay?" Logan asked, and she looked up to see him standing in the aisle. "You look like you spied a haint," he said in his teasing way.

Shaking off the strange feeling, she smiled and joined him. Inside the house the odd feeling of belonging returned. The great room, with its towering windows, heavy maroon drapes, the patina of pine floors and intricate rugs rang with familiarity. Weak in the knees, she fell behind until she was alone. Or so she thought until a southern voice spoke.

"Beautiful isn't it?"

A woman about her own age in a frilly old-fashioned dress stood behind her. "Yes, it is."

"My name's Victoria Markham. I grew up on this block, my best friend lived here in this very house. Once in a while I manage to tour the house by joining one of the organized groups."

"What was your friend's name?" Irrationally, Rana hoped to learn about the little girl she'd seen.

"Jillian Northridge. Jilly was a dear, sweet child. I cried for months when we lost her."

"Lost her? What happened?"

"She disappeared. Everyone always thought she was abducted."

"But you didn't?" Rana asked, surprised at her own boldness.

"I . . . I don't know what I think. I know that I always felt guilty, like I was somehow to blame. I'd give a pretty penny to know what happened to her, though."

A piece of her dream flashed back at Rana. She, as a small child playing hide and seek in this very yard, laughing and racing into the shadows out back. Looking for a good hiding place while someone counted in the background.

"There you are," Logan said, approaching from another room. "I thought you were lost."

"No, Victoria here was just telling me . . ." She turned to introduce the two, but the woman was gone. "Oh, I guess she had to leave. The strangest thing just happened." As they strolled through the rooms on the ground floor she told Logan about the chance meeting. Then mentioned her experience and the ensuing dreams. "I feel sort of silly taking dreams so seriously, but it all seemed so real at the time."

He shrugged. "I've heard of stranger things. Believe it or not, just the other night on Ripley's Believe it or Not."

She glanced at him, saw his features set in their teasing mode. "Oh, okay. I'm sure it's just my imagination. But what about Victoria?"

"Victoria? I don't see any Victoria."

The docent waited while the group congregated in the large entryway. She gestured up the sweeping staircase, above which hung a crystal chandelier. "Those who would like may follow me to the upstairs bedrooms. I must warn you that you may meet the ghost of a child who disappeared from this house twenty years ago." That's all it took to send everyone hurrying upstairs.

The second bedroom they entered, with its pink curtains and canopied bed, had belonged to a little girl. Rana stepped through the door into the room and on into a grassy yard at twilight. Surrounding trees cast deep shadows and in the distance someone counted in a childish voice.

She began to run, looked down and saw the feet of a child.

"Ready or not, here I come," another child's voice shouted.

Ahead was the old well. She could hide there. No one would never find her. She climbed the rock curb, threw her legs over the edge and dropped into darkness. Falling, falling . . .

Screaming, she opened her eyes to see a ring of people looking down at her.

Logan knelt beside her. "Rana, are you all right? What happened?"

When she tried to sit up, he touched her shoulder. "No, stay there a minute. Do you know what happened?"

"No . . . I was . . . I saw. No, I'm not sure." If she related the experience he and everyone else staring down at her would think her crazy.

In a few minutes, he helped her to her feet. "Logan, I have to do something."

"What?"

"Where would I go to find out about a child who disappeared twenty years ago?"

For a moment he appeared puzzled. "Well, I suppose a newspaper office or a library if they have copies of the local newspaper. Why?"

"You're going to think I'm crazy, but I think I know what happened to that little girl."

"What little girl?"

"Victoria told me about her friend who disappeared from this place a long time ago and was never found. That would be the ghost the docent talked about."

"Ah, Victoria, the woman who wasn't here. And surely you don't believe in ghosts. That's just a ploy for tourists."

"I'm not sure what I believe. But if you won't go with me, I'll go by myself."

"Of course I'll go with you, if only to keep them from putting you away when you tell your story."

Frustrated with his attitude, she left the room, not looking back to see if he followed. Nevertheless, she was happy to find him behind her at the bottom of the stairs.

In the rack inside the door, he pulled out a map of Galveston. One of the ads there was for a cab company, and he used his cell phone to call them. She was grateful. It might have taken her a while to come up with such a quick solution.

Thirty minutes later they were going through the archives of the local newspaper. It didn't take long to find the story about Jillian's disappearance. And it took even less time for Logan to reconsider her story when they read that the last time the child had been seen was when she and her friends, including Victoria Markham, were playing hide and seek in the yard of Jillian's house. According to the paper, the children couldn't find Jillian. Thinking she'd probably gone inside, they went home because it was getting dark. When her parents discovered her gone, it was presumed she had been abducted. Since no ransom note was ever received everyone believed the worst. That she had been taken by a pedophile or a serial killer.

The children, including Victoria Markham, had been unable to tell the authorities much.

"I think I know what happened to Jillian," Rana told Logan. "And before you say anything, I'm not crazy. I'm perfectly sane."

He shrugged and waited for her to go on.

"She's in the well out back of the house."

"How can you possibly know that?"

"She showed me. I can't explain it any better than that. It can't hurt to look, can it?"

"Well, *we're* not going to look. We'll go to the police and tell them. They can look."

"Logan, do you really think they'll listen? You don't even believe me. Worse, I can't explain it myself. Somehow I've been chosen by her ghost, or spirit, or whatever, to find her."

"What do you suggest we do? We can't go digging around in an old well on private property for the bones of a child. There's all kinds of trouble we could get into for doing that."

"I know, but what else can we do?"

She took his hand. "Come on."

At the front desk of the newspaper office, she asked if anyone knew where the Northridge family lived.

"Oh, I'm sorry, hon," said the plump receptionist, "they passed away. Shame too, they never found out what happened to that darlin' child of theirs."

Rana turned to leave, then halted. "Wait a minute. Do you know Victoria Markham?"

"Why, yes. Sad story there, too. Victoria was so wrought up about Jillian's disappearance she had a breakdown. She's a recluse, lives all alone in her folks' house over near the old Northridge place. That's where it happened, you know. Everyone was terrified for months thinking we had us a serial killer. But thank heavens no more children disappeared."

"What's Victoria's address?"

"I'll write it down for you, but it won't do no good. She don't talk to no one."

Rana smiled. "She'll talk to me." Actually, she already had, but she kept that to herself.

Outside the newspaper office Logan stopped her. "You want to tell this woman about your dreams? Don't you think it'd be better to find out for sure that this little girl is down in that well before you get her hopes up?"

"What do you want to do, buy a ladder and go down there?"

"No, of course not. But I think I know where we can find someone who can do just that."

He called another cab and told the driver to take them to the nearest fire station. It took a while, but Logan finally convinced one of the men on duty to get permission to send someone down in the well.

"Actually, I'm going off duty and this sounds just fascinating enough to be worth taking a look," the lanky young fireman told them. "I'll make a phone call. You wait right here."

A couple of hours later, Logan and Rana waited anxiously with a crowd gathered around under the trees out back of the Northridge House. Word must have gotten around, no doubt courtesy of the newspaper receptionist.

"All I can't figure out," Rana told Logan, "is if Victoria is a recluse how did she appear to me this morning?"

"Oh, that's all you can't figure out, huh? That was probably a ghost too." He laughed when she gave him a poke in the ribs. "Tell me, do you often talk to ghosts, cause I have to tell you that will take some getting used to."

The inference caught her up short. "Never before. Why?"

"Well, I thought that if we're going to get serious about each other, I'd like to know what to expect. You've got to admit it's pretty spooky."

Before she could react, a shout went up from the direction of the well. One of the firemen held up a hand to quiet the crowd.

"Listen, folks. It would be best if you all went on home now. I can tell you that we've found a body, and it looks to be a child. We ask that you respect her privacy. I'm going to call the coroner now so he can handle this. You'all can come to the funeral and pay your final respects."

Everyone began to drift away, murmuring to each other.

Logan gave Rana a hug, and she whispered, "Now we can tell Victoria." She paused, looked up into his face. "Are we going to get serious?"

Before he could answer, a woman approached. "You're the ones who told them about Jillian?" she asked.

Rana recognized the woman as the one who hd approached her earlier that day at the Northridge House. "Yes. You're Victoria, aren't you?"

The woman grabbed her hands, tears in her eyes. "Thank you so much. All these years I've felt so guilty over allowing someone to take my best friend. She must have crawled down in the well to hide when we were playing. At least we know what happened to her now. Thank you so much for finding her and giving us all peace."

"You helped," Rana said.

"Me? How?"

"Well, when you told me your story this morning, I must have connected it with my dreams and that's how I knew she was there."

"This morning?" Victoria widened her eyes. "I never saw you before this minute. I surely never told you anything. Are you sure it was me?"

Rana glanced up at Logan and he raised his brows.

"Oh, yes. It was you," she said.

Together they watched Victoria walk away, then he smiled down at Rana. "Now, about my question."

"You sure you want to get mixed up with someone who is visited by ghosts?" she teased.

"Very sure," he said, and kissed the tip of her nose.

Velda Brotherton has been writing for twenty-two years, beginning as a columnist for several newspapers. She moved from there to working as a feature writer for one of the papers, and her first historical column was born. That column continues to be published every week. A column about the lost communities of the Boston Mountains in the Ozarks is published in *Life in the Ozarks*. As co-founder of Northwest Arkansas Writers Workshop, she helps new authors hone their craft and occasionally mentors. Velda was a 2008 Willa finalist, and lives in the Ozark National Forest near Winslow, Arkansas.

The Flying Fuquas
By Jerrel Swingle

O don't know exactly how it happened.

I, Felix Fuqua, founder and *pater familias* of the world-renowned high wire troupe, the "Flying Fuquas", am, at this moment, lying face down on a cable less than one inch in diameter some two hundred feet above the ground. I am sweating and in pain.

It might have been a sudden sharp gust of wind. It may have been an unexpected tremor in the earth's crust. It might have been the stupid Channel 6 news helicopter that insisted on hovering overhead. Or, more likely, it might have been the result of some diabolical machination on the part of my swinish son-in-law, Alberto, who, I'm sure, is in league with the devil.

But whatever it was, the sad fact is that the small braided steel cable upon which I was performing high above the ground suddenly whipped under my feet and threw me off balance.

I am not a "Flying" Fuqua despite our publicity. Flying right now is the furthest thing from my mind. I am desperately holding on in mid-air with one hand and two legs. The other arm has been temporarily disabled with a dislocated shoulder. In addition, I have a painful abrasion on my ribcage which occurred when I threw my arm over the cable as I was falling. Cold sweat is beading on my forehead from the pain. My expensive performance shirt is ripped.

The cable is stretched between two buildings, both twenty stories high and about 600 meters apart. (This in a

151

country where a twenty story building is considered a "sky scraper" and of which they are immensely proud.)

I had personally checked and double checked the moorings. Everything was secure as it should be. Members of my troupe were stationed at both ends, including my beautiful, beloved daughter, Dominique, and her asshole of a husband, Alberto.

This has never happened to me before. In a split-second, I was thrown off. I threw my balance pole away. Despite my age, my still cat-like reflexes saved me. I grabbed the cable with my good hand and quickly lifted my legs into a locking position around the wire. What now?

An enormous crowd of fans has gathered below urging me to fall. I can hear their gleeful chants. We are The Flying Fuquas, but that was not meant to be taken literally. I hope my balance pole that went pinwheeling through the air as it fell has cracked a few unsympathetic skulls down there.

So, why am I dangling here with gravity pulling me to certain death? Because I'm stupid, that's why. I'm getting older, and, as I age, I've discovered that gravity has gotten much stronger, making this an even more stupid conceit. But, against my better judgement, I allowed myself to be talked into this, although I have to confess personal ego had a lot to do with it. Who did the talking? Alberto, that's who.

It was Alberto's idea. This demonstration was supposed to be a teaser, a lead-in to pull the curious to our regular performances with the Tinkling Brothers Circus, an entertainment enterprise that appeals to the public's perception of traditional American circus, with all the required elephants, clowns, sexy animal trainers, and trapeze artists.   (It's an overblown outfit, but the pay is good.)

"Just imagine," Alberto had said, with appropriate dramatic emphasis. "The founder of The Flying Fuquas, risking his life in a public display of derring-do. It should bring to the circus hundreds of the thrill-seeking public, and thus provide us with increased income." Alberto possesses a gifted tongue. Which is one reason I invited him to join our troupe a year ago. Another reason is he is a gifted performer in his own milieu.

I first saw him doing hazardous routines on a tight wire with a one-horse carnival in rural New York. He drew large crowds with his juggling and headstand routines, some simultaneously.   I could see immediately that he had talents that would add an exciting new element to our shows. So, after a little preliminary haggling about salary, I hired him. Big, big mistake. I should have known better. I hadn't considered character.

Unfortunately, this vermin is now married to my beautiful daughter, Dominique, who fell for him almost on the day he was hired. She proclaimed and still proclaims undying love for him, though I don't know why. I treasure her, but her judgement in men leaves something to be desired. He began cheating on her shortly after their elopement marriage. An elegant bareback rider became the next victim of his lust. To my continuing shame, I couldn't tell Dominique, though I desperately wished to do so. She would have hated me if I had.

So, now as I hang here two hundred feet above solid concrete and asphalt, sweating and in pain, I look at the safety platform about seven meters away and whose face should I see? It is Alberto's. He is holding out his hands in a fake gesture of assistance. He is smirking, although he is trying to hide it. Dominique is behind him and can't see her husband's features. She is lucky. I can tell she is near tears.

She is pleading. "Hold on, Papa! Hold on!"

Next to Dominique is Andre, the strongest flyer of our group and my most trusted associate. He doesn't like Alberto either. Thus, there is reason to hope. I pull myself forward, inch by painful inch, shinnying as on a vertical rope, but with only one hand and both feet, this time horizontally.

They say that when is one on the verge of eternity, one's life flashes before one's eyes. And, as I pull myself along with searing pain in my disabled arm, sweat beginning to trickle into my eyes, I find, thinking back, that that aphorism contains an element of truth.

Among my more disturbing memories, I recall Alberto unleashing a horrendous fart in the middle of one of our intricate trapeze acts. It disrupted the entire routine.

It must be understood that trapeze requires concentration, timing, and precision. Flying through a cloud of burrito-fueled methane does not conform to those requirements. I thank God we were practicing with a net. Dominique thought it was cute. I didn't.

Among my many other mistakes in judgement, I allowed him to oversee the design of our posters and handouts since I was preoccupied with other business matters at the time. Dominique, my precious motherless daughter, insisted that Alberto could help us. He had, she insisted, an amazing artistic talent. I cannot refuse her. She is so near and dear to my heart.

I didn't see the finished products until after they were printed and distributed.

In glorious color and in the largest typeface available, they proclaimed "THE FLYING FUQUAS, starring the daring ALBERTO CAPPULINO with DOMINIQUE." Further down it also says (in much smaller type) "Also starring Felix Fuqua, Master of the High Wire." I was immediately tempted to strangle him in his sleep.

I am pulling myself along, painfully, inch by inch. The sun has passed midday. The TV copter hovers above me, taping my potential demise for the five-o-clock news. The crowd below is shouting cheers and a variety of obscenities. Safety is a bit closer. Alberto holds out a hand. Helpful? I find it hard to trust him. He is grinning.

Dominique, unaware of her husband's duplicitous nature, is imploring. "Hang on, Papa! Hang on! We will help you."

I'm trying, damn it, I'm trying!

But as I struggle for life in the here and now, my mind insists on going back to unpleasant memories.

At one point, I tried to relegate him to solo performances, some on the ground. It hadn't taken much imagination to realize he couldn't work as a member of a trapeze team. But, once again, Dominique implored. "Please, Papa! You are crushing his artistic spirit." In her innocence, she didn't realize that his spirit was not all I wished to crush.

The bastard steals my beloved daughter. He's responsible for numerous casualties in the troupe. Michelle is currently in a neck brace, and Paul still sports a cast on his left leg; all due to Alberto's ego. I also find the filthy pig helping himself to bonuses out of our proceeds when no one is looking.

I can't fire him because Dominique loves him and always pleads tearfully on his behalf. How can a loving father go against his only child's wishes? So Alberto remains a member of The Flying Fuquas, a painful carbuncle on the backside of what was once a premier circus act.

As a result, we acquire the humiliating sobriquet of "The Flying F***-ups" in the circus world. We are, however, still in great demand in anticipation of spectacular aerial accidents. It draws in disaster-seeking customers, somewhat as NASCAR and "American Idol" do. And our current reputation is all due to Alberto Cappulino. Am I grateful for our popularity?

No.

I'm now about to reach safety. The air is warm, and I can smell my own sweat. I am getting weaker. Alberto reaches out his hand as if to help, but when our fingers almost touch, he draws back about an inch. The others don't see this. They think he's trying to help. No. He is teasing. This happens two more times. I am gritting my teeth and cursing under my breath. He smiles. The bastard is smiling!

Once more I struggle to move forward and extend my hand for help. The crowd two hundred feet below is waiting in breathless anticipation. Alberto pretends to assist. He is holding out his hand. Andre is behind him. Dominique is kneeling to one side, wringing her hands.

My mind and conscience suddenly succumb to the ultimate evil. I realize I'm consigning my soul to Hell, but

I'm tired of this crap. I tighten my grip on the cable with my legs. Thus anchored, I lunge forward and grab his wrist. I pull. He is off balance and begins to tumble past me. His eyes are wide with fear.

Goodbye, Alberto!

Dominique is screaming. The crowd below is screaming. Alberto is screaming.

Andre grabs my arm and pulls me to safety.

I lay there on the platform gasping for breath and trying to cope with the pain in my shoulder. I ask Andre if he can pull the humerus bone back into its socket. He plants one foot in my armpit, grasps my wrist and pulls hard. It pops back into place and the terrible pain immediately subsides.

I know I should be more concerned about Dominique and the demise of her beloved Alberto than in the condition of my shoulder, but at this point I can't summon up the necessary sympathy. She has collapsed in a hysterical heap and I don't wish to look down at what's left of Alberto. I hear sirens from below. Probably paramedics. I don't think they'll be able to revive him. I must remember to say a few Hail Marys the next time I go to mass.

It has been two years now since that unfortunate incident. Dominique finally recovered from her tragic loss long enough to marry Andre, a move I heartily endorsed. He is a good man, unlike his predecessor.

I have retired from active participation in our team's performances and, under my expert management, we have reclaimed our reputation as The Flying Fuquas, one of the finest acts of high wire and trapeze in the entire circus world.

In a strange twist of fate, we have been booked to perform in the same city where the late Alberto came to his untimely end. We have been here three days and the Tinkling Brothers are enjoying sold-out performances due in large part to our presence.

Last evening, in a nostalgic mood, I left the hotel and walked several blocks to the spot where Alberto landed on that unfortunate afternoon. The citizens of this small city decided to memorialize the event (since they have little else to memorialize), and erected a small granite monument where they scraped him off the concrete.

Tonight, there is a Smiley Face spray painted on the stone. I wonder who could be capable of such a despicable act?

Jerrell (Jerry) Swingle (*Adam and Arthur*) is a retired art teacher who, post-retirement, has pursued a life-long interest in creative writing—humorous short fiction, poetry, and essays. He has since had work appear in *Sweetgum Notes, Applecart, eClips, Fantasy Gazetteer,* and *Woman's Corner e-zines,* in *Storyteller and Good Old Days* magazines, *America's Funniest Humor, Missouri Teachers Write, Good Old Golden School Days, Cuivre River Anthology, Echoes of the Ozarks,* and *Well-Versed.*

Maurice's Gift
By Patty Stith

When I was a kid, only bad people had tattoos—a tattooed woman—a heathen of the worst kind. Nowadays it's no big deal. My sixteen-year-old niece had a cute little daisy permanently etched on her toe. Many indigenous groups in the world maintain elaborate, intricate rituals surrounding tattooing and consider it a rite of passage. As the Project Director of an educational program that celebrated the unique cultures of Alaska and Hawaii, I saw hundreds of examples of magnificent tribal art adorning my friends and co-workers. I met some of the most incredible and talented tattoo artists in the United States.

Naturally, I had to have one.

But, I can't even commit to a lipstick color. How could I decide on something I would carry with me for the rest of my life? Something I felt strong enough about that I was willing to undergo hours of pain to achieve. I pondered. I asked everyone I knew. More than once. It became a community project, discussed over morning coffee and greasy Thai food lunches.

At last, the inspiration came from my ten-year-old nephew. Concerned that the stray kitten in his neighborhood would be hit by a car, he wanted to catch it and give it a home. The answer to all things cat was to call me, Aunt Petunia . . . aka "The Cat Whisperer." That's when I knew a cat tattoo was the answer to my quandary. Simple and quite puny compared to the spectacular tribal art my Samoan and Tongan friends sported, yet perfect for me.

The waiting list for the tattoo parlor recommended by friends was four months. Lots of time to rethink my decision. I can honestly say the only reason I followed through was because if I didn't, the entire community had wasted their time on tattoo deliberations. The humiliation of chickening out would be too great.

In order to undergo the needle and ink, I had to fly seven hundred and fifty miles from my home in Barrow, Alaska to my second home in Anchorage. With great trepidation, I boarded the plane and resisted the urge to ask the flight attendant to leave the beverage cart within arm's reach. After researching the possibility of tattooing under anesthesia, I discovered sobriety and consciousness were required during the entire process of inking one's body.

Mesui T'aui, Tongan national, and an extraordinary specimen of walking Polynesian tribal art, was about to inaugurate me. Compared to him and the work he did, my little kitty was embarrassing. I sat on the table, barefoot with my pant leg pushed up to my knee, listening to Mesui explain the process. As we talked, the needles bit into my skin. The image slowly formed. Light gray nose.   Dark gray whiskers. Shadowy cheeks.

Then the eyes. Intense, green and alive.

What started out as few black lines sprung to life. The spirit of my long lost, cuddly, lovable, adoring cat, Maurice—space cowboy, gangster of love—was no longer *only* in my heart. Mesui stopped what he was doing and called several other artists into the room. They stared at my ankle.

"That's creepy, man," Laird with the long red hair and soul patch said.

"Ats teally thool," said Liza with the studded nose, ears, eyebrows, tongue and lips.

"She said, 'That's really cool.'" Mesui translating "pierce" to English for me.

"It's like you now have a guardian with you at all times," Miss Fairy Tattoo said.

Admittedly, it was pretty dang cool and I was thrilled. Everywhere I went, people stopped me and asked where I acquired such awesomeness. Proudly, I told them; although, I was troubled by it. Maurice's spirit was trying to tell me something. Was I being haunted by the ghost of Feline Past?

Over the next couple of days, I was two degrees off center. Nothing was exactly right. I sent a mass e-mail to all my friends with my new cell phone number, but mistyped and was off by one digit. Osso Buco without the veal shanks is just carrot soup and the German chocolate cake that took hours to make was dreadful without the sugar. Something was catawampus.

Two nights before my return to Barrow, I lay in bed at my Anchorage house pondering my offness. The January night was cold, but the crisp, fresh air so pleasant I opened the bedroom window slightly. The full moon cast birch-tree-branch shadows on the wall, dancing in the wind.

A loud screech from under my window shattered the tranquility. I landed on my feet, heart bursting.

What the heck was that? Lynx, badger, wolverine, fox, grizzly, demon?

The screeching continued. I grabbed the shotgun from behind the bedroom door and cautiously went downstairs. Why? I have no idea. Usually I stay in bed with my head under the covers praying for bumps-in-the-night to go away. The icy blood in my veins kept me in steady supply of goose bumps. Downstairs, the horrible sounds intensified. I turned on the outside lights and illuminated the yard, apparently upsetting the howling creature because the growls, pitiful cries and screeching redoubled. I opened the door and used the beam of my flashlight to investigate the dark recesses of the yard. No bears huddled under the yard light. No moose. Nope, not a lynx. Sasquatch didn't attack. The shrieks seemed to emanate from under the porch. The critter couldn't be too big, if it were hiding there. So, bravely, on a cold Alaskan January night, I ran barefoot in my jammies across the snow to do a quick search. A tiny, white ball of fur, no bigger than the snowflakes falling around my head, screamed at me. All I saw was white fur and tonsils.

A blanket. Food. Water. Warmth. That's what the kitten demanded.

I ran back to the house, depositing the shotgun on the couch, and snatched up a quilt. Afraid the kitten would be very shy and take a lot of coaxing to come inside, I grabbed shoes and a jacket. No need.

When my nephew had asked my advice on how to catch the kitten, I told him to hold out his finger. Cats can never refuse extended digits, and must sniff. Not sure why, but try it sometime. It always works.

Following my own advice, I stooped in front of the steps and held out my index finger. White ball of fur crawled out of its spot to smell and nuzzle its nose against my hand and I was able to scoop it up, wrap it in the towel and bring it inside. No scratching. No hissing. It snuggled against me to steal my warmth . . . and my heart.

Upstairs, I offered the baby some tuna. How twenty ounces of kitten can consume six ounces of tuna and still want more amazed me. The afghan I threw on the floor invited napping. It curled up, white fur against bright blue yarn, and started taking its pre-nap bath. When it looked at me, full eye-to-eye contact, the green eyes of my tattoo stared at me.

Maurice brought me a kitten.

After a visit to the vet for shots, I purchased a kennel and called the airline to confirm passage for the kitten. The vet informed me that I was the proud mama of a sweet, little girl kitty. I named her *Avu*, which means "sugar" in Inupiaq, the native language of Barrow.

Flying in Alaska with an animal is always a challenge. The flights between Anchorage and Barrow are on combi aircraft—carries people and freight. Passengers board from the back of the plane because the front is partitioned off for cargo. There are seventy, crammed-together seats available. During the winter, for some unknown reason, the flights to Barrow are rarely full, but Avu's first flight was packed. The morning flight had been cancelled and those passengers forced to wait at the airport for eight hours until the next flight showed their crankiness. Storing a kitten under the seat in front is a challenging task under ideal conditions. On a plane filled with angry passengers and grumpy flight attendants, the feat becomes staggering—especially, in a middle seat. The person by the window was a disgruntled scientist headed to Barrow to study the effects of climate change on permafrost. Miss Aisle Seat was a depressed woman returning home after six weeks in a drug rehabilitation program.

Turbulence filled the short leg between Anchorage and Fairbanks and the flight attendants were unable to serve the abbreviated drink service of orange or cranberry juice. The tossing about did nothing to improve the mood of the passengers. Once in Fairbanks, the plane usually cleared out, as many travelers considered it north enough. Not the case on Avu's first flight. The departing passengers were to be replaced with stranded Barrowites longing to return home. So many, in fact, the flight was overbooked. The forty-five minute boarding in Fairbanks stretched into an hour . . . two hours . . . two and a half hours. The captain wouldn't let the passengers already onboard deplane. With nowhere to walk and no smoking allowed, the already restless passengers began to squirm.

My concern was focused on Avu. Poor little thing, stuffed in a bag under the seat. As soon as we landed, I pulled her out and held the kennel on my lap only to be chastised by the flight attendant. Since I tend to ignore most authority figures, I kept Avu on my lap while the other passengers deplaned.

Miss Aisle Seat glared at me when I bumped her while removing Avu's kennel. Mr. Disgruntled Scientist groaned when my elbow dared to cross the armrest. Avu let out the tiniest of mews. Considering her hungry protests when we met, her meekness amused me. I unzipped the kennel to stick my finger in and rub her cute, little chin. She grabbed it and pulled my entire hand into the soft-sided bag. I chuckled and started talking to her. The lady in the seat in front of me turned around to see what was going on. She gasped when she saw the adorable green-eyed, white fluff ball. A little girl wearing a pink hat, sitting two rows in front of me, heard the word "kitten" and scooted her way through the people milling about. She leaned over Miss Aisle Seat, who muttered something about people learning how to control their children. She wanted to hold her. We weren't going anywhere, so I didn't see the harm.

Hawkeye Flight Attendant stomped down the aisle to stop me from taking Avu out of her kennel. As she swept past the little girl, she bumped her, sending her pink hat onto the floor. Bald. The little girl standing in front of me with expectant, joy-filled eyes had no hair. The backs of her hands were bruised from what looked like insertion points for IVs. The flight attendant instantly mellowed. Miss Aisle Seat moved over so the little girl could have better access to Avu and Mr. Disgruntled Scientist took the kennel and laid it at his feet.

Her name was Tiffany. She was returning to Barrow after receiving treatment for leukemia in Seattle. Avu crawled into her arms, past her shoulder and nibbled her ear. Tiffany made the most delightful sound . . . a child's laugh. The aisle cleared as she carried Avu, cradled in her arms, up and down the rows of the plane so everyone could meet the kitten. The grumpy, angry, agitated crowd smiled, laughed and talked to Tiffany. Avu purred and offered an outstretched paw to the stonehearted people who weren't immediately touched by the scene. Within half an hour, Tiffany and Avu worked a miracle. Several of the passengers on the plane, offered to stay overnight in Fairbanks so those people who must be in Barrow that night could board.

When the plane finally took off again, headed farther north, Avu was safely tucked under a seat two rows in front of me.

Patty Stith worked for many years as a technical writer and editor in Alaska. A native of Arkansas, she returned to her childhood home to pursue a writing career in fiction. She is currently marketing a romantic suspense novel set in the dreary, arctic winter of America's northernmost community and is writing a contemporary romance set in Santorini, Greece.

SAVANT
By Rochelle Wisoff-Fields

*T*ravis Winnery moved into the house next door in 1967, the summer I turned fourteen, on a muggy Sunday afternoon in mid-July. Sitting on our front stoop, I closed my June issue of "16 Magazine" and watched a slender woman heft one box after another from a U-Haul trailer. Not lifting a finger to help, he lounged in the grass with his St. Bernard. What a lazy bum! But a cute one, nonetheless.

Always on the prowl for a good looking guy who would find me irresistible, I decided the time had come to introduce myself. With pretended confidence, I sauntered across two lawns. Crouching beside him, I waved my predatory hand in his face.

"Hi! I'm Audrey. My mom named me after Audrey Hepburn."

Closing his eyes, he turned away from me. Only the dog acknowledged my presence with a cursory grumble. My pride smarted more than a tad.

Unwilling to give up, I edged closer. "You know. The actress. She was in 'Roman Holiday'? 'Breakfast at Tiffany's?' What's your name?"

"My son's name is Travis. He's shy."

Had she not introduced herself as his mother I might have guessed her to be his sister. Her ocean-blue eyes looked like his only her long lashes were enhanced by a heavy coat of mascara. She had the whitest teeth I'd ever seen and her smooth blonde hair, parted down the middle, gleamed like one of those models in the Breck Shampoo ads.

I extended my hand. "Audrey Reubens."

"Peggy Winnery, pleased to meet you, Miss Reubens."

Without stopping to filter them through my adolescent brain, I let my thoughts gush from my mouth like rain from a rusty gutter. "What's wrong with him? Is he retarded or something?"

"Yes."

Wishing I could yank out my tongue and wrap it around my neck like a noose, I clapped my hand over my mouth. I imagined myself suspended in mid-air before plummeting, like Wylie Coyote, to the bottom of a cliff in a distant poof. At the same time, my short-lived dream of showing up at school on the muscled arm of a drop-dead-gorgeous football player fizzled. It joined other fantasies such as being Paul McCartney's girlfriend or Little Joe's first romantic interest to live beyond one episode of Bonanza.

Once more I demonstrated my erudition. "But he looks normal."

Undaunted by my ignorant comments, Peggy laughed. "Normal' is a relative term. His body is normal for a seventeen-year-old and his mind is normal for a five-year-old."

Squatting beside him, she put her arm around him. "This is Audrey. She's our new friend. Can you tell her hello?"

His azure eyes fluttered open and he flashed a shy grin. "Hi—Audrey. This is my doggie Buttercup."

"Hi Buttercup."

I held out my hand. She snuffed and gave it a swipe with her drooling slab of a tongue. I wiped her slobber on my shorts, trying not to gag.

"Audrey!" My father yelled from our half-open front door. "Get your lazy butt in here and clean your room!"

My face heated and I bid a hasty goodbye to the newcomers.

Later, I chattered away to my mom as I peeled carrots. "He's so cute. It's a shame he's a retard."

"Audrey Lynn Reubens! I wish you wouldn't use that word."

"What word? 'Cute?'"

Every Sunday evening my mother filled the pressure cooker with a roast, carrots and potatoes to be eaten on Monday. At the same time Dad would grill steaks on the patio. My stomach growled in hungry anticipation of my two favorite meals.

"Dammit, Gloria, it's sweltering out here." Dad hollered in a voice I'm sure our neighbors recognized as the Bob Reubens Sunday afternoon broadcast. "Bring me some ice water before I melt."

Mom handed me a sweaty glass. "Take this out to your father before he blows a gasket."

"Gloria! Are you listening?"

"Don't get all bent out of shape." I slammed the back door behind me.

Dad's face turned brick red. "I'll teach you to smart off to me."

I ducked his raging hand. In his frustration at missing his target, he grabbed my long hair and yanked. I screamed which appeased his wrath, at least for the moment.

Turning to avoid further confrontation, I rubbed my stinging scalp. I saw Travis sitting on the ground in his back yard watching us, his eyes brimming. I swallowed my own tears of humiliation, forced my heavy lips to smile and waved. His mouth puckered and his brows knit into a single unit.

I spent the next two weeks helping our new neighbors get situated. What could be more fun than rummaging through someone else's treasures? I loved Peggy from the beginning.

One Tuesday, she invited me to stay for supper. "Nothing special. Just burgers and fries."

Mom, a bookkeeper for a foam rubber company in the West Bottoms, usually did not get home until six. Every Tuesday she met with four of her women friends for an all-night game of Mah Jhongg. Dad, a fry-cook, at a local greasy spoon, worked the nightshift, leaving me, for the most part, to fend for myself. Any meal that didn't come from a can or an aluminum sectioned dish with a foil covering was okay by me.

Travis and I raced each other to the table, our arms loaded with condiments. He set down the ketchup with a triumphant smile. I dropped the pickle jar. It rolled across the floor and shattered against the table leg. Grabbing a napkin, I knelt to mop the brine when Peggy touched a tender spot on my arm. I flinched.

"Ouch!"

"Audrey, how'd you get all those bruises?"

Despite the heat and humidity I wished I'd worn long sleeves. "I'm a klutz."

"Oh I see."

Avoiding her raised-eyebrow stare, I finished gathering broken glass. I wrapped it in the napkin and escaped to the kitchen. Finding the trash can, I dumped my pickle mess. Turning to go back to the dining room, I ran smack-dab into Peggy who stood over me, arms folded.

"Travis told me. If you ever need a friend to talk to, I'm here."

"No thanks." I hurried past her, blinking back my embarrassment.

A painting hanging on the dining room wall caught my attention. I didn't remember unpacking it. Eager to distract her, I pointed. "Groovy picture! It looks just like you. Who painted it?"

"Me." Travis, who rolled a Matchbox car over his burger, grinned and poked his chest with his thumb. "Mommy just put it up today. Vroom! Vroom! You like it?"

Peggy snatched the toy. "Didn't I tell you my Travis is a special boy?"

"But you said he has the mind of a five-year-old."

"He does. But for some reason, known only to God, he paints like Rembrandt. The doctors call it 'Savant.'"

"Sa-VAHNT." I repeated the word. It sounded regal. Almost musical. "Do you think he'd paint a picture of me?"

"Ask him."

Right after supper, Travis set up his easel. He changed; kind of like Superman bursting out of a phone booth. The impatient child who couldn't wait five minutes for an ice cream sundae disappeared and the serious artist who would spend weeks on one painting took his place.

The following Saturday, Mom and Dad had a fight; the worst I'd seen. They threw things at each other, shouting obscenities. When he wrapped his hands around her neck, I couldn't stand it. I tried to pull him off. His knuckles smacked my cheek. Fiery balls of light danced before my eyes.

After he left for work Mom and I settled into our routine of eating popcorn and watching "Saturday Night at the Movies" as if nothing had happened. I curled up on the sofa with an ice pack pressed against my face.

"Mom, why did you marry him in the first place?"

She turned off the television. Her huge brown eyes took on a faraway cast. From the coffee table, she picked up a frayed leather-bound album and opened it to a photo of a group of soldiers and young women in shoulder-padded dresses. "World War II. A picnic our Hadassah ladies group gave for the Jewish soldiers at Ft. Leonard Wood. Your daddy was a handsome man. He made me laugh."

"You fell in love with him because he made you laugh?"

"I didn't fall in love with him. He begged me to marry him. I was twenty-seven and no one else was asking." She clawed at her neck as if trying to brush off a bug. "I danced with another man at our wedding reception. Dad flew into a jealous rage. Guess you could say the honeymoon was over."

"I'm never getting married."

"You'll change your mind." She clicked on the TV. "I just hope you do better than I did."

Monday morning Mom went to work as usual, leaving me alone with Dad. He had become more sullen than usual; remorseful, I suppose. It didn't matter to me how many times he apologized. I hated him.

I chugged down a glass of Tang and ran next door to sit for my portrait.

"Can you make me look pretty?"

"You *are* pretty," said Travis.

I tugged at my frizzy hair. "My hair's too curly."

"I like curly hair."

"I wish my hair was straight like your mom's. Then I wouldn't have to iron it."

He giggled. "You're silly!"

I stared at his angelic face. He rivaled every one of my TV idols when it came to looks. I fantasized what it would be like if he weren't—different.

"Don't put this in the picture, okay?" I pressed my hand over my eye.

"He shouldn't hit you. It's not nice."

"Nobody hit me, Goofus. Can I see it?"

I stood and shuffled behind him, ruffling his flaxen hair with my hand. Flipping the painting before I could see it, he shrank back. "Don't! Don't call me Goofus!"

"I'm sorry." I knelt beside his chair. "That wasn't nice, was it?"

Touching my bruised cheek, he gazed at me, his cobalt eyes wet with tears. He leaned forward and our lips met. I closed my eyes, forgetting his low IQ and breathed in the scent of English Leather. His mouth, soft and warm, enveloped mine.

Pulling back, he chewed his lower lip. "Did that hurt?"

Friday morning my world tilted sideways and then turned inside out.

I shuffled into the kitchen to forage for breakfast. Opening the cabinet, I took out a box of Cheerios. Dad had eaten most of them. He sat at the kitchen table beside an open window wearing only striped boxer shorts and a white undershirt over his ample body.

"It's about time you got your fat tukhus out of bed."

I tugged a strand of his chest hair and made a face. "Look who's calling whom 'fat.'"

Glaring at me over his newspaper he slurped his coffee. "Going next door to play with your imbecile boyfriend?"

My chest hummed with indignation and my stomach turned flip-flops. "He's twice the man you'll ever be."

"Why you little tramp!" Grinding his teeth he stood, rolled up his paper and whacked a stinging blow across my face.

I forced a deliberate smile, determined not to let him see me cry. "Ha. Ha. Didn't hurt."

I hurled the cereal box to the floor and stomped to the living room. Cheerios crunched under my bare feet. He followed me, huffing, fuming and breathing every epithet in the book. I don't remember anything after he picked up a lamp from the end table and lofted it over his head.

A week later I came to hooked up to an IV, my head pounding out the beat to "Wipe Out".

I had to fight to make sound come out of my mouth. "Mom? What happened?"

"Thank God!" Her puffy eyes behind her rhinestone-studded sunglasses said she'd been crying for days. "That horrible retarded boy went berserk and attacked you and Daddy with a lamp. I hope they lock that moron up in the loony bin where he belongs and throw away the key."

"No—no, Mom. Not Travis."

The police came to the hospital to question me. I told the truth. I had to. How could I let Travis live out his life in one of those awful places when his only crime had been to save mine? Dad should've gone to jail, but it would've been pointless since he didn't remember the incident at all. In fact, he didn't remember anything or anybody, not even Mom and me.

The stranger who replaced my angry father was sweet-tempered and gentle. It took me a while to get used to his pleasant smile and the way he kissed my forehead every morning. He lost weight and, eventually, Mom truly fell in love with him. Not exactly the "happily-ever-after" kind of love, but a comfortable, foot-massage-every-night kind of love.

Peggy and Travis moved away before the doctor released me from the hospital. I felt cheated but I understood. Even though Mom dropped all charges, the stigma would always be there.

Two months later I sat on our front stoop watching our new neighbors unload furniture from a moving van. No boys; only a redheaded girl who waved and skipped through our overgrown grass. Her freckles danced across her nose when she smiled. Flashing a mouthful of gleaming braces, she bounced to a stop on our sidewalk.

"Hi! I'm Paula. I'm fourteen. What's your name? Can I use your bathroom? They haven't turned the water on at our house yet."

I stood and opened the front door. "Audrey. Sure, come on in! Hey! We're the same age! Do you like Star Trek?"

"Best show on TV next to 'The Man from U.N.C.L.E.' I love Mr. Spock!"

After she emerged from the bathroom I showed her my room.

"Nice picture! Looks just like you." She pointed to the portrait hanging over my bed. "But why do you have a black eye?"

"A reminder."

"Of what?"

"My first kiss."

"That must've been some kiss!"

Rochelle Wisoff-Fields lives in Belton, Missouri with her husband Jan. Together they've raised three sons. A formally trained artist who attended the Kansas City Art Institute, she enjoys painting word pictures.

She's a member of Ozark Writers League and Kansas City Writers Group. Her first novel in a series of three, *Please Say Kaddish for Me,* has received praise, but is still looking for a home.

A Change of Mind
By Ann Holbrook

"*O* feel trapped, without hope or options." Dianne sighed and twisted a strand of long, silver hair around her left forefinger.

Becky nodded. "Me, too. I don't see any way out of our predicaments."

Lounging against fluffy pillows on queen beds, the middle-aged ladies drank coffee in their comfortably modern hotel room.

"If my grown children don't start handling their own marital problems instead of coming to me with them, I'm going to run screaming like a banshee down our street!" Dianne flailed her arms in the air for added emphasis. "It's just too much."

"That has to be tough," Becky said. "I'm also very exasperated. Dealing with my in-laws' chronic health issues is stressing me to the max. My husband's siblings are useless; they always have some lame excuse why they can't help out. I'm really afraid of what lies ahead."

"I know that fear about the future. My man's cholesterol has skyrocketed recently because of work issues. But then, he comes home and thinks I'm supposed to automatically take care of his over-active libido." Diane shook her head. "Heck, after babysitting three grandchildren under the age of five, I'm worn to a frazzle. Guess I'm just plain weary of the caregiver role in general."

"You know, I'm glad we managed to get away for this brief shopping and relaxing trip," Becky said. "However, we need to talk about why we're really here — to make plans for our final, *permanent* escape."

"Well, let's see. We could try hanging ourselves," Dianne said. "I've heard it's effective and simple; we just need some rope and a chair."

"Eewww, I don't want my eyes to bug out. Plus, I've already had too much trouble with my neck." Becky absentmindedly patted her spiked, copper-colored hair. "What about cutting our wrists with sharp knives?"

"Yuck, I can't stand the sight of blood. It makes me feel faint, which wouldn't do in an emergency situation."

"Guess you're right," Becky said. "Well, there's shooting ourselves with a high-powered gun."

"Nope, too messy. I'm an organ donor and that might clutter up the works."

Dianne got up, poured another steaming cup of coffee, then resumed her lounging position. "You know, there's always the drug overdose. People have done it for decades."

"Yeah, but I never had any respect for those 1960s hippie types and their psychedelic drugs." Becky wrinkled her nose. "I sure don't want anyone to put me in the same category with those people."

"Well, I've thought about taking some sleeping pills, fastening on a gas mask with duct tape, and breathing carbon monoxide from a canister, Kevorkian style," Dianne said. "However, I've always had trouble with tape sticking to itself in the wrong places. There has to be an easier way."

Becky sat up and stretched her flabby torso. "All this death talk is making me hungry. Let's order in a stuffed pepperoni-and-jalapeno pizza."

"Sounds great. My taste buds need a little jolt. After you call for the delivery, I'll turn on the television. We gotta watch our shows."

During the next couple of hours, the ladies pigged out on spicy pizza, drank more coffee, and watched HGTV.

"Some of those interior designer guys are really cute," Becky said. "Too bad they're gay."

"Yes, such a pity," Dianne nodded, undoing the hook fastener on size fourteen crop pants. "That reminds me. While we're out shopping this evening, I need to find a skimpy negligee. I want my man to have a marvelous, lasting memory of me after I'm gone. Hmmm, I just hope he doesn't have a heart attack while we're making love and die before me."

"That would sure muddle up your plans, huh? You know, I've been wondering about death by drowning, but I don't know much about it."

"Since I can't swim, my family would assume I'd been murdered," Dianne said. "They'd launch an all-out, time-consuming investigation. No, it's not for me."

"You're right. Besides, those jellyfish scare me. I've always been afraid of something stinging me all over like that."

"Speaking of drowning," Dianne said, "I need to go get rid of some of this coffee."

She went to the bathroom, but came back a minute later with a frustrated look on her face.

"What's wrong?"

"The stupid toilet won't flush. That's just great!"

"I'll call down and report it." Becky put on her reading glasses, punched the number for the front desk, and relayed the problem.

"They're sending one of the maintenance guys up right away," she said.

A few minutes later, three knocks sounded, followed by a husky, "Maintenance man."

Becky opened the door and nearly dropped her coffee cup. Standing before her was a handsome, muscular man, probably in his late thirties, with a dark tan and long, black ponytail. An Old Navy T-shirt fit snugly around his biceps and abs. Blue jeans, work boots and a large red tool box completed his manly ensemble.

He pointed to his nametag. "Hi, I'm Steve. I picked up the work order for this room."

"Uh . . . yes . . . please come in," Becky said, with a sweep of her free hand. "You . . . it's . . . the toilet's evidently not wanting to flush."

"I'll check it out." Steve said hello to Diane, then sauntered into the bathroom. He promptly lifted the ceramic lid and looked into the tank. "Right there's your culprit. The chain to the flapper is broken."

As soon as he bent down to pull a new chain from his tool box, the ladies looked at each other, grinned, and wiggled their eyebrows up and down.

With biceps bulging, Steve fixed the problem within minutes. He locked his tool box, grabbed the handle, and stood.

"Around my house, stuff breaks and seems to stay that way a long time," Dianne said. "If it's not the kitchen sink, it's the clothes dryer, or the lawn mower. Too bad you don't live in our town — I'd hire you."

"I understand, but I like my job here."

"Don't you get tired of working on dirty toilets and sinks every day?" Becky asked. "I think that would drive me crazy."

"Naw. You see, things aren't always what they seem. I'm a Master Plumber and an electrician, so I get paid well. But, there's more to me. I'm also an outdoorsman, musician, and writer. I love my life."

Dianne's eyebrows peaked. "We have a true Renaissance man in our midst, Becky."

Steve's smile showed perfect white teeth. "I look for the silver lining behind the dark clouds. It's always there. Things have a way of working out for the best if we have faith and truly believe they will."

"It's been a real pleasure meeting you, Steve." Dianne stuck out her hand and he shook it. "You've given us a lot to think about."

"Yes, I believe our particular toilet broke for a reason," Becky said. "You were supposed to come and bring us a new perspective on life."

"Just doing my job." Steve touched fingertips to forehead in a salute. "Have a great day, ladies," he said before exiting.

The two women stared at the door for a few seconds before looking at each other.

"Do you think we've been a bit hasty in wanting to do away with ourselves?" Becky asked.

"Perhaps. Maybe our lives aren't so bad after all." Dianne shrugged her shoulders. "At least we have families who love us; many of our mutual friends can't even claim that much."

"Yeah, and we do get away for coffee or shopping once in a while," Becky said. "Guess those things count for something, huh? Hey, speaking of shopping, do you want to go look for those racy negligees now? I'm sure our husbands would want us to at least buy those."

Dianne laughed. "Boy, for potential 'suicidettes', we've suddenly decided life is worth living after all!"

The next day as the ladies were leaving the hotel, Becky told the female manager, "Please say 'hi' to Steve for us."

The manager's expression changed from business smile to perplexed frown. "Steve? The only employee by that name worked in Maintenance."

Becky and Dianne nodded.

"You must be mistaken. Steve died three months ago in a boating accident." Her face softened. "He sure knew how to live life to its fullest, and was always trying to help people realize what a precious gift life really is. But how did you ladies know him?"

Ann Holbrook lives in Northwest Arkansas. She has been published in *The Storyteller* magazine, *Writing on Walls* anthologies, and *Echoes of the Ozarks* anthologies. Ann is working on an inspirational book for cancer patients and their families taken from her experience as a twelve-year ovarian cancer survivor.

Sack of Suckers
By Russell Gayer

"When the dogwoods are in full bloom the suckers are on the shoal." That's what the old timers used to say. Snagging (or grabbing, in hillbilly vernacular) has been an Ozark tradition for generations. The fish were cleaned, chopped, stuffed into jars, and canned using a pressure cooker. Patties, or 'fishcakes', were made by adding egg and a little flour to the canned fish and frying in a cast iron skillet. Sadly, man-made lakes and lack of access to prime spawning locations have made grabbing a thing of the past. Only a few old timers remain, and their number dwindles each year. This is my attempt to capture the essence of that tradition and honor those who loved it.

It was about nine o'clock when Pug's old Chevy pick-up popped over the crest and onto the floor of the War Eagle Mill Bridge. The heavy wooden timbers made a cloppity-clop noise under the tires as the truck crept slowly toward the center of the bridge.

Billy Stafford was draped over the iron rail, slinging his hooks up river and jerking them back down. Four or five fish tails were sticking out of the top of his five gallon bucket.

"'Bout to get a bucket full, Billy?" Pug asked as he rolled to a stop.

"Well, there's a few in there," said Billy as looked over his shoulder. "Who's that you're hauling around with you today?" he snorted, gazing at Choc and Harry. "You know these yellow suckers don't like the smell of pipe smoke. I believe I'd left that old codger at home."

"I think you got that backwards, Billy," mumbled Choc.

He always spoke with his teeth clamped together whether the pipe was in his mouth or not. The result was a unique presentation of what had formerly been known as the English language.

"When they smell this pipe smoke they come swimming up the river like piss ants to honey. Then all I got to do is have Pug to take 'em off my hooks and get Rip to sack 'em up."

"One thing for sure," said Harry, in the hoarse, raspy voice that had become his trademark. "There's never a dull moment when you're fishing with Choc."

"It takes two people just to see after him," he chuckled, stuffing his Velvet tobacco tin back in his overall bibs after rolling a cigarette,

"Well, we better get off the bridge before a car comes," said Pug. He eased his foot off the clutch and guided the old truck down into the dirt parking area across from the mill.

They crawled out of the cab, untied their cane poles and headed down to the gravel bar. It had rained a little the night before. The river hadn't come up much, but the water had a good dingy color. There was a good current, but not too strong. Conditions were just right to entice suckers into migrating up river for their annual spawning ritual.

Pug had made several sets of grabs the night before, each consisting of nine single hooks about five inches apart. He had neatly wrapped them around a large piece of Styrofoam for tangle-free transportation. This also minimized downtime when a new set was required after hanging up and breaking off.

They each tied on a set of grabs, adding sinkers above and below the hooks to keep them close to the bottom as they traveled downstream over the rough gravels.

Choc waded in almost to his knees. "Water's pretty chilly," he reported.

Slowly he swung his long cane pole up river, depositing his hooks as far up stream as possible. About halfway through the first drag Choc felt something hit his hooks and gave a quick jerk. Moments later he wrestled a two pound sucker onto the gravel bar.

"There's the first one!" he crowed.

It wasn't long before both Harry and Pug were pulling in fish too. Pretty soon the three of them had eight or ten yellow suckers and a couple of red horse lying on the rocky shore.

"Guess we ought to sack these," said Harry, dragging another fish to the bank. "Don't want 'em to start drying out." He reached into Pug's old canvas hunting bag and pulled out three burlap feed sacks.

"That's a good idea," said Choc, cane pole bouncing from the weight of his latest catch. "You sack 'em, Rip. Me and Pug will keep you busy."

Harry distributed the fish in the three sacks and placed a large rock on the neck of each to keep them from drifting away in the current. Then he sat down and rolled another cigarette. By the time he had it finished and lit two more suckers had landed at his feet.

Within a couple of hours the three anglers had totaled thirty-five to forty fish and the action had begun to slow down.

Pug and Harry waded out of the water and sat down on the gravel bar to rest. "Got some good fried apple pies here if you're hungry, Choc," said Pug.

"I'll be out in a minute," answered Choc, continuing to swing his pole up river. Suddenly he felt a hard thump against his line. The end of his sixteen-foot pole bucked violently. Z-z-z-i-ippp his line sang, shooting up river.

"Got a big 'un on!" he hollered, fighting to maintain control of the cane pole.

Choc staggered forward a few feet, attempting to improve his leverage on the wild beast at the end of his line. Without warning the line went slack, quickly followed by an emerald flash as the huge red horse darted downstream and behind him. In less than a heartbeat the fish had encircled his knees and made a mad dash for deeper water.

The line jerked taunt, yanking Choc's knees together. For a brief second he tottered like an inverted pyramid, arms flailing in a vain attempt to keep his balance.

Ker-splash! He disappeared beneath the rolling current.

The next thing Pug and Harry saw was Choc's wide brimmed straw hat floating down stream. Choc clambered to his feet, pipe still clenched firmly between his teeth, and watched in dismay as the large red horse surfaced in front of him, waving its crimson tail as if to say goodbye.

"Looks like the big 'un got you," chided Harry, between bellows of laughter. "Minnie's gonna wonder why you didn't wait until you got home to take a bath."

"Want me to get you a bar of soap, Choc?" laughed Pug.

Choc mumbled and grumbled some unpleasantries as he sloshed ashore, pulled his billfold and tobacco pouch from his overalls and lay them on the ground to dry in the warm April sun.

Pug retrieved Choc's hat and after a few more merciless jokes about baptism by red horse, he and Harry picked up their poles and started fishing again.

About his second or third cast Harry pulled out a nice sucker. He untangled his hooks from the fish and tossed it on the gravel bar. "Hey Choc, while you're sitting there sunbathing why don't you sack that fish for me?"

"It would be my pleasure," said Choc, with a gleam of mischief in his eyes.

By now, it was late afternoon and all three sacks were heavy with fish. "Boys, we're gonna have to quit after a few more drags," warned Pug. "My old cows are gonna be waiting at the milk barn."

"Well, I'm ready any time you are," said Harry. They waded ashore, secured their grabs to the cane poles with electrical tape, and gathered the remainder of their tackle.

"Rip, why don't you carry the poles and rest of the stuff," suggested Choc. "Me and Pug can carry these sacks of fish to the truck?"

"That suits me," answered Harry. "It's always nice to have somebody tote your fish."

Choc watched Harry scoop up the tackle and head down the trail. "Let's pull one on Ol' Rip," Choc whispered to Pug.

"What ya got in mind?"

"Let's take Rip's sack of fish and dump 'em back in the river, then fill the sack with rocks."

"Big brother, you are ornery and lowdown. Let's do it."

Harry was leaning against the side of the pick-up rolling another cigarette when Choc and Pug arrived with the sacks of fish. "It sure took you boys long enough," he said as he lit his smoke. "Thought I was gonna have to send out a search party to look for you."

"Your darned old fish are awful heavy," snorted Choc. He and Pug gently lowered the burlap sacks into the bed of the truck to avoid giving away the rocky contents to their unsuspecting brother in-law.

All the way home Harry continued to perfect his version of Choc's bath in the river. Most of the actual facts flew out the window. Minnie was going to hear how a six-inch river chub had almost drowned her husband.

Choc just sat in the middle of the bench seat smoking his pipe and occasionally nodding in agreement. From time to time he would look at Pug and give a little wink. "You're right, Rip," he agreed. "There *will* be a good story to tell."

Before long they pulled up in the yard at Choc's house. He and Harry quickly unloaded their tackle and poles and Choc drug out his sack of fish. "I believe that sack is yours, Rip. It was a lot heavier than mine or Pug's"

"That's what happens when you catch the most fish," Harry stated proudly. "I told you boys this morning that I was going to catch a whole sack of suckers."

"Well, dump it out on the ground and let's see how many you got," urged Pug.

Harry's sack hit the ground with a thud. Grasping the bottom of the sack and heaving upward he dumped half a wash tub of rocks out at his feet.

Harry stared down in disbelief, cigarette dangling from his lower lip.

"Well, Rip," said Choc, grinning from ear to ear, "who's the sucker now?"

Russell Gayer is a Fourth generation Ozark native, residing on the original family homestead in northwest Arkansas. He enjoys writing poetry and humorous short stories. His work has been published in Ozark Mountaineer magazine and on-line at www.frontiertales.com.